Jetta
The Calling Series (Book 2)

By Deana Zhollis

This book is a work of fiction. Names, characters, places, and incidents are the product of the author's imagination or are used fictitiously. Any resemblance to actual events, locales, or persons, living or dead, is coincidental.

ISBN 10: 0-9821215-1-2
ISBN 13: 978-0-9821215-1-1

Published by Night Before Day
http://www.zhollis.com

Cover Design by Kelly Carter
http://www.madspiderstudio.com/

To my family and friends who have supported me. And especially, in loving memory, to my father—my number one fan.

TABLE OF CONTENTS

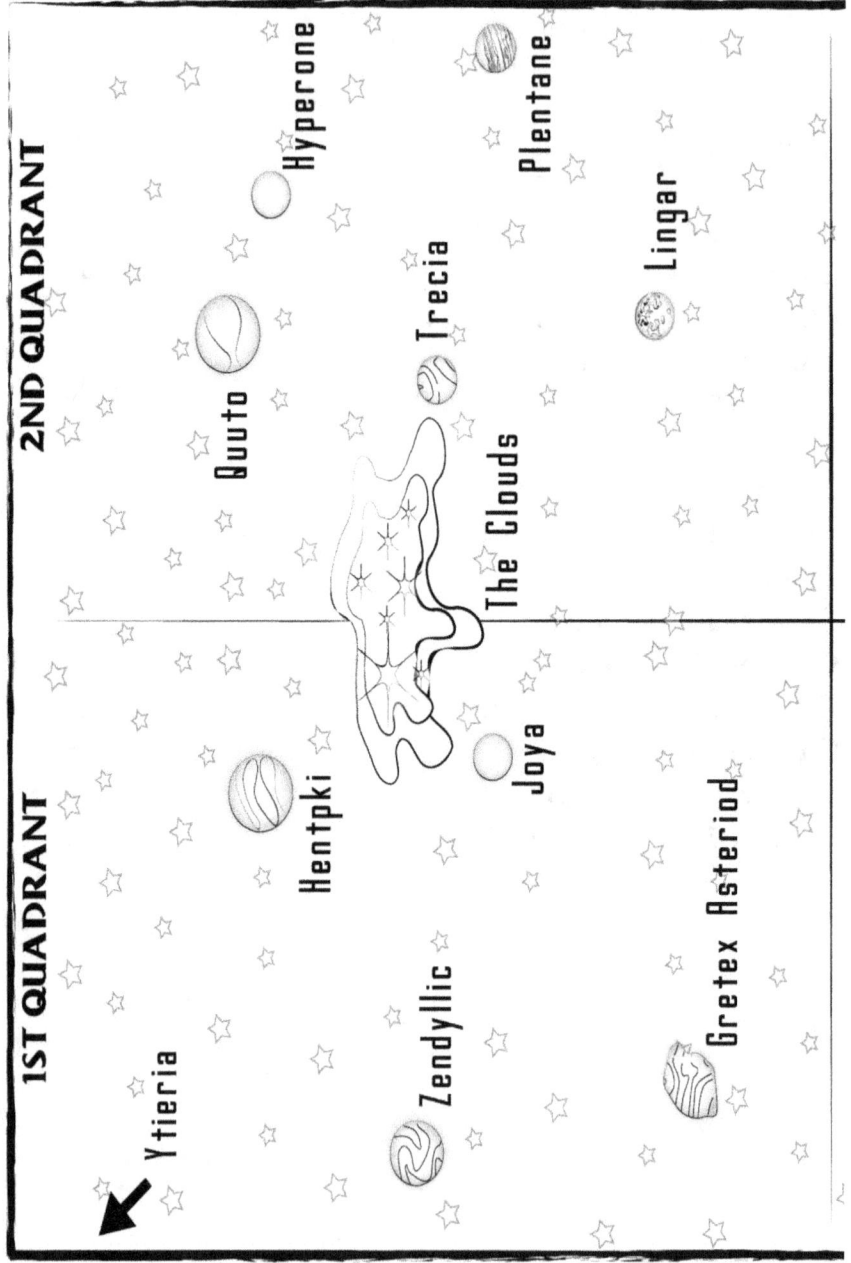

4TH QUADRANT

Deluxar

Ivka

Urlanshoran Star

Xarthren

Tokane

3RD QUADRANT

Jancso

Xen

Uten

Isdol

Ayalum

Chapter 1   Reuss

It reeked!

The nauseating smell made my nose run, and I was miserable. The deeper I traveled through the Renavid district, the fouler the odor became, and the night air seemed to bathe in it. I turned away from one of the sewer vents, tugging at my skirt as I passed, but the foul mists surrounded me, escaping from cracks in the street and permeating the darkness.

Steic! Why did Vrang want to crypt here anyway? All this trouble just to find his sequestered nook didn't seem worth it. The drome I had taken to Renavid left me at the outskirts, stating that it had "insignificant data on the area for further travel." Sure. Dromes were filched more than the high-rise residences in Renavid. The Counsel couldn't risk losing any more. That's probably why Renavid was never on Hentpki's map. The planet wanted it forgotten.

I continued walking through Renavid's unlawful grounds with buildings structured to look like colorful corals growing up from a seabed. It was a popular style a hundred cycles ago, but now it made the district look slummy. The lighting was poor as well. Most districts were lit up as if it were daylight, but Renavid remained dark, a black blotch on Hentpki's surface. And presently, it was darkness where I was spending most of my life.

"Over here, sweetness! Take a bite from me!" Someone shouted.

I hurriedly crossed the street, ignoring the bawds who waved at me and flashed their lights for sexual hire. There were more whores in the streets tonight because of the Seven Days Fest, which was a constant reminder to everyone of Imperial TeNeil's youngest son's kidnapping during the war. The kidnapping had inspired the Four Quadrants of intergalactic species to join together and defeat the Xarthren species. It was a terrible war that lasted five cycles too long, yet we continued to celebrate it. Festive laser-lights flashed through the sky on the main street, and two-seater galers skimmed the air, their headlights bright, and their operators directing them to no particular destination.

Slipping into an alley, I welcomed the darkness again. The open night was filled with too many festive lights. Just a few more streets and I would be there.

I wiped my wet nose again. The Counsel continues to say that they are "in the process of rectifying the sanitation problem," but they had been saying that for cycles.

At least the smell kept my mind occupied. I didn't want to concentrate on the sexual hunger that I had stupidly let heighten within me. I should have started searching for Vrang to quench me as soon as I felt the yearning. Thank Suphyz that I didn't have the complete anatomy of a Wendh. If I did, I would have been locked up in a soundproof room right now, completely insane, or in incarcerated for committing some demented crime. But tonight was one of those rare nights that I was thankful for my Human half.

It was a handy tool that the Goddess Suphyz had bestowed on us, this hunger. Wendhs were a slave to it right after puberty. Before The Calling, Wendhs could quench their desire with anyone they please. But after hearing that song, Suphyz's Calling, they had no choice. The song brought about an uncontrollable need that only could be quenched by joining with a True Mate. Whether I would ever hear The Calling or not, I didn't know; I wasn't fully Wendh. If I were, I wouldn't be trudging through this forsaken district, seeking out Vrang.

I stopped at a door, looked at the corner edge and spotted the Reuss's symbol. The thieves' mark was barely distinguishable in the caked dirt, but I didn't have to search for the hidden entrance. Suddenly, screaming, I felt the ground slip under my feet. My shrieking was muffled as I hit a gel bag, knocking the breath out of me.

I heard someone chuckle as I scrambled hard, trying to get out of the bag. "You're losing your touch, Jetta. You tripped twenty alarms coming here."

A Quattor stood over me with his four huge arms crossed in front of him. His head barely brushed the ceiling. It was somewhat rare to see one of his species since most of them resided in the Second and Fourth Quadrants of the eight galaxies. His name was Karplus.

He held out one of his huge hands and helped me out of the bag, continuing to laugh.

I glowered at him. "I wasn't trying to be stealthy."

"I know," Karplus chuckled, his mass of muscles unstirred. He turned around, still laughing, and I noticed that he had shaved the small, black patches of hair that grew sporadically on his head, making his blue skin smooth and shiny. He marched down the steel tunnel, and I regained my composure and followed him.

We made our way to the Reuss's hideaway with only the sounds of Karplus's chortles to keep us company. I knew he wasn't laughing at my fall; he was laughing at my accent. I had been offworld for seven cycles and had been speaking the common galactic tongue fluently for six cycles, but I still hadn't gotten rid of my Simple accent.

"Will you be feasting tonight?" I asked, trying to change the subject. Laughter seemed to never end with Karplus. "It's quite lively out there."

"Why would I want to celebrate the memory of a Wendh who's been dead for ninety-three cycles?" the Quattor snorted, "especially one of royal blood? What have the elite ever done for me?"

Karplus's answer was typical of all deviants. Anything or anyone associated with wealth was quickly snubbed.

I lowered my head slightly. On my home planet, I was considered regal, but that was another life. Yet I still felt as if I were also being condemned and categorized with those who led lucrative lives.

I changed the subject again. "The Reuss did a good job in sealing the cracks in this place to keep out the smell. This district stinks!"

"The Counsel will take care of that," Karplus joked and ducked his head a bit more as we passed through an area with lower ceilings.

I laughed and returned his sarcasm. "Yes, any time and very soon now."

Karplus turned around and flashed his toothy grin, then stopped, stepped over something, and waved with two arms, indicating that I could safely pass. It was most likely a trap he had disabled before we could continue.

"How long will you be on shift?" I asked, looking for the trap, but I couldn't see anything. Whatever it was had been cleverly camouflaged to resemble the floor.

"I'm not on shift," the Quattor answered laconically. "Tagg is."

Nothing more had to be said. I understood.

We passed Tagg by the controls, light flickering off his sleek, black body. His coal-black eyes reflected no white whatsoever as they remained fixed steadily on the mechanics surrounding him. The Wendh was beautiful. To me, all Wendhs were. But they despised me for being what I was.

If I were more like my brother and sister, perhaps Tagg would have accepted me more readily, but then again, my siblings were more Wendh than I was. I couldn't even mentally communicate with my own mother. I wasn't telekinetic or telepathic or tele- anything, a blessing the Goddess Suphyz gave to every Wendh. But She had given me nothing.

I glanced back at Tagg, who never looked up from his console as we walked by. His toned arms and tentacles constantly moved as he surveyed the district. I tried not to stare at his naked chest, rippling with strength. A thick chain hung low on his abdomen, weighted down by a medallion with the imprint of the royal child on it. I knew it was his good-luck piece, which a lot of Wendhs wore, reminding them of the triumph over the Xarthrens, and the mystical royal--the Imperial's youngest child--whose death was celebrated.

I took in a deep breath as I stared at Tagg's strong tentacles that he lengthened now and again absentmindedly to help maintain the console before quickly reabsorbing them back into his body. He had hair down the center of his head, a rare trait for a Wendh. Most Wendhs were bald or had thick cords of cartilage that lay like braids.

One of Tagg's feet tapped as if to an unheard beat, while the other mashed buttons sporadically on the floor. He had first alerted of my presence in the area, and bluntly refused to investigate after seeing me on his screen. He sent Karplus instead. Tagg despised me like a bad taste in his mouth, only acknowledging me when he had to. He was one of the main reasons I had left the Reuss.

Turning my back on Tagg, I looked at the door that Karplus was quietly unlocking. There were so many locks, codes and lasers on it that it took him several minutes to open and bypass them all. The wait was uncomfortable only because I knew Tagg was silently cursing me beneath his calm, collected demeanor.

"Be at home," Karplus said, allowing me to enter the room first, for which I was grateful.

The Reuss gang was all inside, lounging around on bags and boxes or anything else they had found abandoned in buildings or in the street. Six different species lay about like dregs of society instead of the intelligent, professional thieves that they were. If it weren't for the security of their surroundings, one wouldn't have known that they were proficient in what they did.

"Jetta!" A voice shouted, and I nodded at the Joya who acknowledged me. His beak barely moved when he spoke, but it was always parted as if he were breathing through it instead of the two holes below his eyes. The Joya rustled his white and black feathers, which grew only on top of his head, and flexed the small muscles on his arms and chest. He vibrated this way when showing enthusiasm or excitement.

I smiled at his warm greeting and noticed the cloudiness of his green eyes and yellow pupils. I couldn't see the patch, which was probably hidden under his shirt, but I knew he was inebriated.

"Coming back to work for us, are you?" The Joya clapped and smoothed down his feathers. "Tired of the clean, easy cates?"

"No, Soang," I answered, following Karplus. "Just need to pay Vrang a little visit."

Soang laughed, knowing exactly why I was there and, to my embarrassment, announced it to everyone. "It's quenching time, Reuss! Simple's back!" Soang began to mock my home world, which was not technologized.

"Simple!" the others joined in.

"Did you get here by animal or mineral? Aieeooo!"

"And how is our craving tonight, Jetta?" a voice mocked my accent.

I gave them a wry smile as I opened the only other visible door in the room. There were probably four or five other unseen doors or exits to this small room. I knew this only because I, too, had been a Reuss one cycle ago. Reuss's believed in several escape routes, and most of them were deeply hidden. I stepped through the door and silently closed it behind me.

Vrang was inside, his hairy arms around an overly dressed female who looked out of place. She wore a gossamer dress and expensive slippers that glittered in the dimly lit room. Her hair was laced down her back and her skin was flushed pink with arousal. The stylish outfit was too luxuriant to be worn by a bawd. Besides, Vrang wasn't into paying for sex. So, she had to be high-caste.

The giggling female stopped smiling when she noticed me in the room, and then glared at me. Vrang finally turned around as her laughter abated.

"Jetta," he breathed, releasing the female in his arms, quickly forgetting her.

Sensing competition, the female's jealousy kicked in. "Who is this?" she pouted, her flushed skin turning from pink to red.

"Get out," Vrang said softly, still staring at me.

"What . . .?"

The female was shocked, though she shouldn't have been. She was an elite anyway, possibly hanging around ruffians for some quick thrills. Knowing Vrang, I was sure he treated her badly, and she probably liked it--when he controlled it. But if she didn't obey . . .

Vrang shoved her, and she slipped and fell to the floor.

"Get out," he repeated, his annoyance rising.

She took the warning and got up, straightened out her dress and stomped out of the room. I allowed her to bump into me as she went out the door, taking her rudeness more with humor than an act of aggression.

"Jetta," Vrang repeated gravelly, walking towards me, the black slit in his red eyes dilated as he stared intently into mine.

He was short, with stocky arms and legs like all Lingars, whose home world was in Second Quadrant. Rolls of hair grew on his arms and the backs of his legs, while the rest of his body was covered with small, gray stumps that protruded like round scales. The larger mounds were mostly on his head and outlined his slit mouth. He walked as if he were stomping insects under each step, bouncing sharply up and down.

He didn't ask why I was there; he already knew. Pulling me to him, he began nipping at my neck with his many, tiny teeth. It was ticklish, but before I could laugh, he flung me on the table and jumped on top of me. I had made sure that I wore a skirt with flexible undergarments so that we could take care of my need as quickly as possible.

"Came for this, hmmmm?" He breathed in my ear as he forced my legs open and stuffed himself inside me. "Want this, hmmm?"

I ignored his comments as I concentrated on keeping my pelvis tilted to receive his many jerky, thrusting motions.

Sex with Vrang had once been pleasurable, but now I was just going through the motions. Vrang was the only Lingar I knew, and Lingars never contracted sexually transmitted diseases. If I made time to find another compatible species that I could join with without contracting a disease, I would have never searched out the Reuss again. But due to my Human side, I can get infected quickly and, thanks to my Wendh side, I would die slowly. Until I found another Lingar, I was stuck with Vrang.

I inhaled the pheromones my body needed that were only produced during this one act. With all the technology in the world, no one has ever produced a drug that would satisfy a Wendh's need for sex. There were some out there, but Wendhs either quickly became immune to them, or they only lasted for a short amount of time. Fortunately for me, I could go at least three months before the hunger became overbearing. A pure Wendh can only endure one month.

Seeing that I was unresponsive, Vrang yanked my hair. "Tough little simple, huh. She can handle this, huh?"

"Stop it, Vrang!" I hissed at him. I hated him pulling on my hair, and I hated when he tried to use sex to annoy me.

"Make me," he said, thrusting harder.

Before I could push him off of me, he released his semen.

"Fleik! You sessling pup! Get your soggy stump out of me!"

Vrang laughed, pulling himself out and adjusting his pants over his thick, fleshy loin.

"Sessling pup?" He mocked my simple cursing. "Such language."

I hit him, and Vrang doubled over with a groan, clenching his stomach.

"I should kill you!" I screamed at him.

I wasn't concerned about getting pregnant. It would take metamorphosing him for that. I just didn't like semen, of any kind, squished inside me, and Vrang knew that. He was doing everything he could think of to anger me.

Something was wrong.

Vrang remained bent over for some time. I took the few minutes to wipe his disgusting, black fleik out of me, grabbing his mistress's costly scarf to wipe myself clean.

"I should kill you," Vrang finally said softly, straightening up.

I looked up to see him pointing his ring at me.

Calmly, I stared at the deadly weapon and continued to wipe between my legs, though inside, my heart was pounding rapidly.

"If you want an heir, Vrang," I hissed sarcastically, "use your mistress. Not me." I threw the scarf at his feet, daring him to react.

Stepping on the scarf, he walked towards me, still holding his ring out. The tip of the gold circlet had a red glint that shined like a fresh drop of blood. I didn't know how many lives that ring had taken or how many bodies had been carved and sliced, but I didn't want to be added to the number.

I stood still as Vrang held the ring close to my face and then swept my feet from under me. I fell on the floor, hurting my backside. Vrang didn't wait for me to recover as he lowered and lunged himself inside me again. Our eyes locked as he pumped, the ring blazing between us. He released himself again inside me, thrusting his semen so that I could feel every disgusting gush. I held my tongue, knowing that my life was at stake here, and not my pride.

It wasn't like him to act this way. Something was eating at him, something bad.

He held his face close to mine, too close. In his anger, he would probably go so far as to kiss me, and I hoped, by not being a willing partner, that I could survive it. Wendhs could not kiss on the lips for fear of death. The chemicals contained in the saliva would turn toxic and kill a Wendh in minutes, but it was proven that the kiss had to be willing, something to do with the type of pheromones released at the time. An unwilling kiss would just make a Wendh sick, but I was unsure about myself, being that I was only half Wendh. I was too weak. A Wendh could only survive a willing kiss with a True Mate, and Vrang was far from that.

Fortunately, he got up. "You do what I like, and when I like it."

I remained quiet as I watched him adjust himself and walk to the corner of the room. Any act of defiance would make him turn around and carve me into screaming pieces.

I grabbed the scarf again and wiped myself clean. I hadn't heard anything out in the streets about Vrang going insane. I couldn't understand his behavior. Well, it didn't matter. Whatever his problem, it wouldn't be mine. Tomorrow, I would find another Lingar. I'd pay for it if I had to.

I quietly walked towards the door, not waiting for a sarcastic farewell.

"Wait," Vrang said brusquely in a low tone. "I'm not finished with you yet."

Steic! I hoped Vrang had already joined with his young mistress several times before getting with me. Lingars had spurts of sexual arousal, and Vrang had six to eight of them.

I turned around and said, "I'm quenched, Vrang. I don't need any more," and then reached for the door.

"I said I wasn't finished." He walked around me and barred my way as his red eyes teemed with exasperation.

He took me again, swirling me around and banging me against the door, and again on the table. That made four. I hoped he had his mistress twice before me. Each time he spurted his semen, and the last time he laughed when he did it.

"Annoyed, eh, Simple?" he derided me.

"Just finish up," I spat.

"You used to love my longevity."

"And you used to respect me!" I shouted.

He fell silent.

Vrang had a soul; he wasn't completely heartless. He just seemed to forget about it sometimes.

He thrust something into my hand before leaping up. "I have a cate for you to do."

Astonished, I stared at the metallic ball in my hand and then tossed it up onto the table. "I'm no longer Reuss, Vrang. I work for Sadotch now."

"I'm not asking," Vrang turned and walked over to retrieve his belt of instruments.

So, this was what was bothering him. Tonight he had a cate.

"No, Vrang. The last time I worked for you, I served two cycles reforming."

"Thirty days," he remarked callously. "You should have kept reminding yourself that you were in virtro.

"No matter how unreal it was, Virtual reforming was still very real to me." I wiped myself a third time and slapped my hand on the floor.

Vrang disregarded my anger. "You were only 'associated' with the reoet crystals. It wasn't like they found them on, or anywhere near you. Your sentence would have been longer if they had."

"If they were on me, I would be dead!"

Vrang shrugged. "Be thankful the season for crime was high that year and the cells were overcrowded; otherwise, you would have served ninety days of six virtual cycles."

"Two cycles were hard enough!" I retorted austerely. "I don't care a fleik what you think!"

He ignored me.

"Ti'senot," I waved the argument away. "I can't do it anyway. Sadotch already has a cate for me." Exhaling with annoyance, I got up and headed for the door again.

A beam of concentrated fire shot past me and branded the air. I bit my lip and slowly turned around.

Vrang lowered his ringed finger and continued organizing his instruments. "I said, I wasn't asking."

"Vrang, please . . ." my voice was a mere whisper. It was a sign of weakness, I knew, but I couldn't stop myself from begging. Whatever Vrang was getting into, I wanted to be at the opposite end of the galaxy when it went down. This wasn't good, and his entire behavior showed that.

"The techchart was programmed for one exchange only." He slipped some rod instruments under the manufactured skin on his arm, which he used for concealed pockets. He would be less suspicious showing more skin in public than bulky clothes.

I looked at the silver ball still on the table.

"I only need eyes on this cate, Jetta. That's all." Vrang sounded almost sympathetic. "Eyes for thirty minutes, peak."

"Then why didn't you use that mistress who just walked out of here?"

His sympathy quickly vanished. "A job well done is a job done repeatedly," he recited. "You have two hours."

He nodded towards the techchart, ordering me to pick it up. I was the only one who could handle it now. If anyone else touched it, it would disintegrate.

I snatched it up. "You should have had it programmed for two exchanges. If I didn't come tonight, who would have taken this on?"

"Two hours, Jetta."

Light suddenly flooded the room, and the high-caste stormed in. "I've been waiting for an hour!" she shouted in Vrang's face.

He smiled maliciously and grabbed her hair, tearing her expensive attire to shreds.

"Stop, Vrang, Stop!" she overly exaggerated. Though she was furious, she did not resist his advances.

I made my exit, knowing that the female would enjoy Vrang a lot more than I had, and glad that he was using up his remaining spurt of lechery on her.

I stuffed the techchart in my pants before Karplus led me out of Vrang's lair through unlit tunnels and winding pathways. Since I didn't have true Wendh sight, he held my hand periodically when the darkness became blinding. I followed his lead, stepping where he stepped, pausing when he did. The Reuss were very cautious. If they were being pursued, their hunters would be killed by these mazes of traps.

Karplus suddenly stopped and gave me no warning, as I felt the sudden prickles on my flesh and saw then a flash of light. I was suddenly wedged between two buildings several stories high. My feet were pressed firmly on one wall, my back pushed against the other, and my knees were stuffed in my face. The wind didn't reach me in this narrow position, but I could still feel the cold. I refrained from moving--the Reuss's training was innate, making me freeze and think.

My choice was to go up or down, and the wrong choice would mean my death. Below me, I heard loud music and festivities, but that wasn't the way. I conjured up the drumming chants that had been drilled into my head during my training to become a thief. These chants were necessary for my survival when I was a member of the Reuss. If I made the wrong decision, my mother would only know I was no longer alive simply because of the time elapsed between communications.

"Be very wise
A Reuss's chant
Or see your demise
A Reuss's chant
Heed very well
A Reuss's chant
And you would revel
A Reuss's chant"

Every song began that way; it was the second verse that always changed, and there were about forty of those.

"On a path to your goal
A Reuss's chant
Never go beneath
A Reuss's chant
Never go left
A Reuss's chant
Or change on a wreath
A Reuss's chant"

A Reuss never turned around, never headed down and never went left. So, which building was on my right? I had to be facing the correct direction when I reached the top, or some beam or light-grid would cook me into dust. I looked for the Reuss's sign, which was right between my feet, sketched on the wall. I was shoved into this position for a reason. If I had moved even an inch, I would have never seen it. The symbol pointed to my left, which meant that was the way I had to be facing to choose the right building. Using my shoulders and feet, I squirmed my way up.

I glanced down between my thighs, wondering how close the light-grid was. It was invisible, at least to my eyes, but I knew it was webbed between the buildings, probably only a hand length away from my previous position. There was another grid on the building that my back was pressed on, so when I reached the rooftops, I grasped the edge in front of me, let my legs slide down until they were dangling, and pulled myself up. As I climbed over to the building's rooftop, I exhaled with relief.

Heading for the outskirts of Renavid, I held up my wrist and spoke into my qCarpus to signal a drome. I had one implanted when I left my home planet. Unlike most in the Four Quadrants, mine was not implanted from birth; therefore, it was in the latest design, with small glistening crystals outlining the vitae symbol--the symbol of life--that comprised everything about me, my entire bibliography, from my biology to my psychology. The style actually made me look like a child, being that it was only seven cycles old. It was programmed to access the intergalactic network secondary to accessing my personal area network. My computer, Bymé, responded in an amiable voice. "There are no dromes available in this area, but I found several available dromes on the outskirts that will not receive my signal."

I had programmed my computer to be female and to offer opinions, making her more personable, though most Beings just wanted their computers to do what they said. I preferred more feedback, and Bymé gave that to me, and more.

"Renavid District, of course," I grumbled. "Thanks, Bymé, I forgot. I'll have to walk."

"Precisely," she answered.

Chapter 2   The Cate

When I finally arrived at my quarters, I took a quick shower and then laced myself with utiq oil, an illegal substance but used frequently by those in my profession. It would keep each skin cell and hair in place while I did this last cate for Vrang.

"Image," I commanded Bymé, who immediately connected to all the appliances in my quarters the moment I walked in.

An exact holographic image of myself appeared in front of me, matching my every dimension.

"Turn," I said, and watched my graphic-clone rotate.

The light in my washroom illuminated the oil on my bronze skin, making it easy to inspect myself. My small, pert breasts seemed more appealing in the image than in real life, and my slim frame glistened. I had braided my hair up and around my head to keep it out the way, though I knew I should cut it. It was better for a thief to have short hair, but I could never bring myself to do it. My hair was my favorite asset. I spread more utiq on the braids and more on my thin legs. It would be just my luck if I left dead skin somewhere on the cate-trail, and my DNA was traced back to me.

"Stop," I commanded, and the image stopped rotating. "Bymé? Do you see anywhere that I missed?"

"No, Jetta. You were very thorough," the computer answered.

I continued to stare at the image nonetheless, and the more I stared, the more it appeared that I was looking into the face of Emera, my mother. I looked like the hybrid that she occasionally transformed into when she used her Wendh blood to its limit. My opalescent black eyes had no whiteness to them like Humans, but shone with the darkness of my father's race. My nails were also black, yet not as sharp and hard as the bone structure of a true Wendh.

"You look like your mother," Primum Inash had said to me during genial meetings, his tentacles enclosed warmly around me.

"Father, you say that about Emariat, too," I said, dismissing his compliments.

"Your brother is male, Jetticia. You're female. So you're more like your mother."

My mother had sent me offworld when I had reached thirty-three cycles, because she wanted at least one of her children to experience the stars that she loved so much. Emera had never left Ytieria, my little home planet so very far away. I was never sure why she just didn't undergo galactic traveling herself and experience all the wondrous technology that her home world refused to utilize. Little did she know how tarnished her bright stars were.

There was a time when . . . but that was at the university. I no longer had to contend with daily taunts and insults from the Wendh students.

Half-breed. Hybrid. Mongrel. Abomination. That's what they called me at the university. That was the time when I had secretly cried to be purebred. Perhaps if I had been more Wendh like my siblings, or had telepathy or something tele-, perhaps I would have been more accepted. My sister's ability was limited, but it still gave her a commonality with other Wendhs. My brother's blood, on the other hand, was fully Wendh, but he looked completely Human. If it weren't for his strength and tentacles that sprung from his sides and were reabsorbed at will, no one would have known he wasn't

Human. His tentacles were translucent instead of black like a true Wendh, which made them appear weak, but his physical and mental strength was a Wendh's equal. I had nothing of Wendh except my eye and nail color.

I would argue with the students that my parents were True Mates just like theirs. It didn't matter that they lived on a Free-Willed planet that refused to practice or ignore The Calling. The Goddess Suphyz loved the Free-Willed Wendhs just as much as those who listened to Her song to find their True Mate. Besides, my father had heard that beautiful song sung by Suphyz Herself, and he went to my mother and mated with her like a Wendh was made to do.

Hearing The Calling for my father wasn't by choice, however. He would have gladly stifled his senses from hearing it by mating with another Wendh and producing a child. But he was Called to my Human mother and transformed her, making her more compatible with his own species. My father forced this need, this hunger, on my mother, forcing her to come to him again and again, or die an agonizing death.

And my mother? She had dreamt the history of my father's ancestors, as a non-Wendh would when joining with his or her True Mate. Through the dreams, she had learned who my father was, learned every aspect of him, and developed his abilities-- the many languages he spoke, the craft of weapon-making, the fighting skills of some of his ancestors, and all of his tele-abilities.

However, Primum Inash didn't finish the metamorphosis, which my mother should have undergone. Instead, he impregnated her before the joining was completed so that she could continue to maintain her Human form. But that didn't matter. They were still True Mates despite my father's choice. He loved my mother, even more so than those students' parents at the university.

I didn't tell my family when I left the university, knowing that they would have been ashamed. Instead, I took to the streets. The next news that they heard about me was when I was reforming for two cycles on the Gretex asteroid for stealing reoet crystals.

"Image off," I commanded, turning away from the memory of my parents. I stood still as the oil dried.

Minutes later, I commanded Bymé to display my image again, and I looked at a stranger in the holograph. Every time I used the utiq oil, it reflected light to make me appear to look like someone new. The female who peered at me now was ten cycles older than I, and she wasn't Wendh. She had brown hair, nails and eyes, and cute circular lips. There was a reddish-gray color to her skin, and green scales glistened slightly on the sides of her face and down her neck. She was Yetanlier, or was she Natanlier? I could never distinguish the difference between the two species.

Satisfied, I got dressed.

I donned a skintight outfit with texture as thin as a membrane, but to the eye it was thick and sleek. My midriff was bare, and I took some synthetic skin and sealed it on my abdomen to form a pocket. When the skin changed its color to match my disguise, I stuffed the techchart in it, along with an inactgun, which was the size of a thumbprint. I carried the weapon just in case I needed it, but I'd never had to use it. Even if I did, it wouldn't harm anyone. It only caused temporarily paralysis. I wasn't a killer, and I wanted to keep it that way.

The techchart contoured to my body so that it did not bulge, and I checked to make sure that my abdomen looked normal. Vrang had some very high-tech devices here. This cate was big. I only hoped that he wasn't lying about me being only eyes. "Thirty minutes," he had said. Just to make sure no one noticed anything suspicious. But he didn't mention the prep time.

The techchart vibrated softly against my belly, and I took it out. Two hours had already passed, and it was ready to tell me my first goal. It shifted slightly and took its sphere form. Coordinates shone brightly against the metallic ball, and I memorized them quickly. I gave it a pat when I was done, and the numbers disappeared. Leaving my lodgings, I signaled a drome.

The drome dropped me off in a secluded park, and as soon as it was back in the air, I took out the techchart again. It showed more coordinates, and I used my qCarpus to signal another drome. I figured I would be doing this for the next forty minutes, so that no one could trace back a thief's steps. I was dropped off and picked up at five more coordinates before the techchart turned colors. Another phase of the plan.

The ball opened up, and inside was a sheer left-handed glove, a thin metal pin and two cornea lenses. Once I removed the wearable items and put them on, the ball displayed a short video. A scene appeared, indicating where I currently stood. Then, the video began to twist and turn through several streets. It gave directions to an apartment and some hallway turns. It repeated several times and then ended with an image of a young female. She was Joya like Soang of the Reuss, with brown and yellow feathers on her head. Joyas were common in the First Quadrant, as their home world was only a few planets away from Hentpki. This one had green eyes and yellow slit irises, which showed no emotion as her face rotated in the ball. Underneath her holographic picture was the word . . . "detain." It glowed brightly before shimmering off.

Detain? Vrang didn't mention that I had to harm anyone. Steic!

I took out the metal pin and eyed it. I partially wanted to turn back and head home, but I was already here, and the cate had to be finished. I kept the pin ready between two fingers.

I looked around, seeing only a few beings walking here and there in the streets. It wasn't unusual to have a techchart. Everyone used them to get around unfamiliar areas or to compact several items for traveling. No one seemed suspicious of me. It draws attention only when someone takes it out too much. I made my way to my destination.

The streets were crowded, and I had to appear ordinary, thus forgettable. Once I reached the building, I waited for several beings to enter and leave before heading to the entrance. With my gloved hand, I placed my fingertips on the smooth plate next to the door. As it opened, I walked quickly through.

"Welcome, Zarre," the computer guest greeted me.

I didn't know who Zarre was, but the finger and palm prints were most likely those of a lowly worker in the building. I headed to the escalators and made my way to the apartment that the techchart showed me. No one was in the hallway when I finally made my last turn. As I walked towards the door, it opened, and the female I saw on the techchart's video screen appeared before me. She was leaving.

My training quickly set in as I pleasantly approached and then passed her. Turning back around, I reached out to touch her with the pin hidden between my fingers.

She turned around with a questioning look.

"Excuse me. Where is the--?" I didn't finish my sentence as I caught her before she went down. She never felt the prick.

"Are you alright?" I feigned concern, continuing to play my part just in case anyone was looking. "Let me help you back into the apartment. Are you sure you're alright?"

The door to her apartment was already closed and locked. I used her hand to open it, though I knew that my glove could have also done the job. Vrang always made sure that every key he bought would open even the most unlikely of doors.

I dragged the female into the apartment and closed the door behind me. Okay, she was detained. Reaching for the techchart, I patted it for my next instructions.

It opened and revealed tweezers and a small patch. I reached for the tweezers first and used it to pick up the patch, which I gently laid on the unconscious female's forehead. She would remain unconscious for several hours and wake when the patch fully dissolved. Now, what?

The ball closed and opened again, revealing its video screen. It showed the female's clothing and underneath that, more coordinates, then blinked out.

I stared down at the female; her breathing was steady. I was her exact size. If I didn't come seeking Vrang for my need, I wondered whom he would have put in my place. He had someone in mind, I was sure; I just happened to be able to fit the part. I turned the Joya over and began undressing her. I took off my own clothes and placed them in a pile by the door. With the same pin I used to drug the female, I cracked it and threw it on the clothes. With a spark, the clothes turned to mist and quickly evaporated. I put on the female's garments and went out the door.

A drome was already waiting in front, its lit surface stating it was predestined and could not be reprogrammed for another destination. Taking no chances, I jumped inside and looked at its coordinates. They were the same coordinates indicated on the techchart. The Joya probably signaled this drome before leaving her apartment. I pressed the button, confirming the destination, and it lifted into the air.

It was some minutes before the drome landed, and I stood beside one of the most expensive hotels on this planet--Hotel Quitimah. I didn't want to continue. What cate did Vrang have here, of all places in the universe? I rolled my eyes and placed my head in my hands. No wonder he picked me for this. I should have known. The perfect pieces to a cate made a successful one. Every player in the cate was important, no matter how insignificant the part was, and so far my part had been easy. I couldn't leave the Reuss vulnerable. They were still my friends.

Releasing my breath, I touched the techchart, concealed in my belly. I spotted several other beings dressed in similar attire as mine and followed them to the back entrance. I was playing the part of a maid or some kind of servant. The Quitimah Hotel was known for its personal touch--it used live servants for its elite guests. How ironic. My mother was a maid before my father made her, and now she's a Primstress of the Olegace Province.

I placed my hand on the glowing plate by the entrance and lowered my head for the retina scan. The lens I was wearing must have been quite expensive, for this scanner was top quality. With some degree of nervousness, I passed the scan and was allowed entrance.

I kept my hand near the techchart. It had grown two small spikes to fit my fingers. When I passed or came to hallways, it pricked my fingers lightly to tell me which direction to go. After a few turns, the spikes pulled away from my fingers and the ball vibrated lightly. I had reached my destination.

The room was filled with lush chairs and sparkling tables. Mechanical devices floated high above dangling lights, waiting to be called upon for any task they were capable of doing. Several servants were gathered here, taking a break, I assumed. This was where I had to watch.

I settled down in one of the chairs and mimicked other servants, watching reports on the holoscreen. Festivities continued on in all eight galaxies, celebrating the victorious war won dozens of cycles ago and the Imperial's deceased son. Image after image of the celebration and remembrance of the elite youth was shown between clips of planets and their customs of the celebration. Finally, the many juxtaposed images ended with the finale of the report: the Imperial TeNeil's home.

The stately stronghold resided in the First Quadrant, where I lived, but several star gates away, on the Wendh's home world, Zendyllic. Its walls loomed high in the sky, covering acres of land and sea. I had seen images of the Imperial's home time and time again, but the structure still amazed me. The camera circled the entire house, showing its magnificence before zooming through the front entrance and winding down large, lit corridors to the formal dance inside.

I used to believe that my parents' house was huge; it was the largest house of the two provinces in the region. However, the Imperial's ballroom seemed to be the size of my father's entire house. It was filled with elite beings dressed in original, classy suits and gowns, sitting or standing in balconies that jutted out over the grand floor. The room buzzed with their voices as an orchestra played on a stage to the right. A platform with a large, lengthy table sat at the front, occupied by Imperial TeNeil himself and his immediate family. Above and behind him, floating in her large elegant chair, was the Grandeur.

The Grand Queen Holen.

She was the grandmother of grandmothers of the royal families that reign in the Wendh's home world. She sat in silence, never uttering a word. No one had heard her speak openly for hundreds of cycles, though privately she spoke to the royal family. Her age was uncertain, even to the Imperial himself, who sat aligned to her Highness.

Imperial TeNeil was a large Wendh, the largest I had ever seen. His strength showed in his eyes and body. His tentacles sprayed behind him to a height that rose several feet above him and his mate, forming the sign of his power; it was a brilliant display. He reflected his power, as it should be of one who had owned the Four Quadrants, eight galaxies, for two hundred cycles.

"What I wouldn't pay to roll around with one of his sons," one of the female servants said, awed, "or even a daughter."

They laughed.

"I don't want the daughter," a male servant said. "Give me the mother herself!"

Roaring laughter filled the room.

The Imperial's mate was named Rasendei, and she was a beautiful being of Utenl lineage of the Third Quadrant. Crystal-like flesh crowned her head and glittered like sparkling diamonds. Her plump body was covered in a long, elegant gown, reflecting her divine nature.

All of the royal family was beautiful and powerful. Being the highest and most puissance of all beings in the universe, the Imperial family's position on Suphyz's Bow of Color was Violet. On my home planet, the strongest mental mind only went up to Green, and that was what I was, though I had no mental abilities at all. I could only imagine the tremendous power that a Violet had.

Imperial TeNeil gazed about at his many guests and the camera looked around as well, as if we were seeing through his eyes. There were more than five thousand in attendance, and more would still arrive.

"The Imperial has outdone himself again this year," a presenter said over the screen of the formal gathering of the elite. "And you can see how his guests appreciate their invitations."

The camera swung over to a room filled with gifts. The total cost of them could probably buy an entire planet.

"Preparations for this Seven Day Fest were planned during the entire last cycle, beginning just one night after the last fest," the presenter explained. "And you can see that the hard work has been well received."

The camera spun around, zooming into the faces of the excited guests. The equally excited servants at the Hotel Quitimah called out names of elite faces that they recognized. It seemed to be a game of who knew more than whom.

The camera then panned back to the royal family, zooming in as close as it could to fill up the holoscreen.

"Vortsi isn't there," a female exclaimed, noticing that the close cousin of the royal family was not in the holoscreen.

"He received The Calling a week ago, didn't you hear?" someone answered.

"That's just a rumor," the female dismissed. "Even if he did receive The Calling, do you think *we* would have heard about it? A Royal in Calling is never told publicly; it's too much of a risk."

"Well, that's the word," the other female insisted. "It's also rumored that he headed for Deluxar, that space station in the Fourth Quadrant, for his True Mate. There's one lucky female in that part of the universe."

"Space Station? Fleik!" the female laughed. "What a rumor. Oh, look! There's Doxmon!"

The holoscreen was filled with the face of the Second Son. He was the most favored with the females and still available.

"I wished he had a Calling for me!"

The Imperial only had seven children: three males and four females, noting that the seventh child, LaSar, was dead. This was a very small number of children for an Elite, but the Imperial's mate couldn't endure bearing more children after the kidnapping and murder of her youngest child during the first cycle of the Xarthren war.

A servant male approached me, smiling, blocking my view of the holoscreen.

"One of the stars must have fallen into your eyes." The male bent over to get a closer look at me.

For a moment, I panicked, thinking that I might have not passed the scan after all. But then I recognized the Reuss greeting.

"And I think the star just flew back into the atmosphere." I replied and stood up to take another seat elsewhere.

Several females giggled at the shunned male, who feigned embarrassment and left the room.

"Can't even work without one of those panting at your legs," one of the females said in my direction.

I nodded congruously and turned my attention back to the screen.

Thirty minutes was all that Vrang said I had to do, and I was back in the comfort of my home. The Reuss who had approached me was also "eyes" and was probably at the end of his duties as well. It was a good sign that he hadn't seen anything yet wrong with the cate. I wondered which Reuss he was, as I couldn't recognize him with the utiq oil on.

A floater came down from the ceiling. "Cleaning needed, suite floor thirty-five, room four seventeen," the metallic voice ordered. This one had a holographic face placed on its round, silver body. Expensive indeed. Most floaters only had two lights for eyes and a blinking third light that flickered when it spoke.

A light beamed at me and three other maids in the room, and then floated back up into its position.

I grimaced. Cleaning!

"Come on," the female who had spoken to me said. "It won't take long. We can come back in ten minutes if we're quick. We won't miss too much of the holo."

Reluctantly, I stood up. I had to play my character.

We loaded up on a hover car, sitting on hard seats. It flew through back tunnels, avoiding the hotel's guest, and passed several other servant hovers as it made its way to its programmed destination. It mounted to an extended platform that went to a closed door, and beyond it, crossed hallways. I followed the servants' example as they snatched up handheld rods that were mounted on the hover. We made our way to the room that we were assigned to clean.

I cursed under my breath as we entered the suite. This was one more incentive to find another Lingar for my hungers. I could see Vrang laughing at me now.

The suite was extravagant; it was the size of three of my living quarters. Streams of gold and ruby cloth covered the entire room, giving it a soft, plumpish look. Nothing seemed out of place to me; even the bed was already made. The servants knew what we had to clean, however, as they headed straight for the washroom. With the handheld rods, they began pointing at everything in the room. I did the same, watching mists vaporize into the air. It wasn't strenuous work, but it was quite tedious.

I began to feel uneasy, and my garment started to feel uncomfortable. I tried to ignore the sensation, but it only increased. Dizziness set in, and I found a place to sit down.

"What's wrong?" one the servants asked. "Not allergic to mist, are you?"

I didn't know. "I just need some air," I assured her. "I'll be back."

I headed for the sleeping quarters and sat on one of the large chairs. The sensation didn't go away, and my loins began to tingle, which clearly identified the problem.

Steic! Did four times with Vrang not quench my cravings? What's wrong with me?

My agitation increased, and I had to leave the room. Back on the platform by the hover car, the sensation intensified. I braced myself against the wall, trying to calm my senses. The hunger was hitting me hard. I debated about one of the males still cleaning the washroom and then quickly put that thought aside. I was on a cate. I couldn't let my guards down now. Steic!

The hunger pangs ached in the middle of my stomach, and I wanted to vomit. I tried getting into the hover, but the hunger attacked me, my insides feeling as though they were being wrenched apart. Doubled over, I turned in the other direction, supporting myself on the wall. The more I continued in this direction, the more it abated. It forced me past the room assigned for cleaning and down the hall to the left, as if to say, "Go this way."

I halted in front of large double doors. The pain inside was relinquishing but was slowly replaced with another desire. I was being pulled towards the doors; an urgent need to open them overwhelmed me. *What was wrong with me?*

I tried to go back the way I had come, but the pain emerged again, demanding to be obeyed. I stood once more in front of the doors.

Vrang. What did he do to me?

I cursed as my hand involuntarily extended towards the door.

What have you done to me, Vrang? I swear I'll kill you!

My hand pressed the panel on the door, and a shock of energy knifed through my body. I felt myself falling . . .

Chapter 3   Interrogation

"She's awake."

The voice reverberated in my head. I clinched my eyelids together and opened them. The dizziness was still there, and the hunger was waiting in the back of my senses. I coughed before examining my surroundings.

I was surrounded by light--no, a spotlight. It held me down by concentrated gravity. Every part of my body was held fast except for my neck and head. It was an uncomfortable feeling. Looking down at the chair, I searched for a weakness in the force, but immediately stopped as I mentally priced the technology's value. The effect of the light gave the chair a gilt-edged look and made the metal appear almost like crystal. I recognized the chair immediately and quickly became uneasy. If I were in the presence of an Enforcer, it wouldn't be in a chair like this. I would be in a crowded room with the rest of the malefactors, waiting for a trial and conviction. But this chair . . . this torment of horrors was, in fact, illegal.

"What the steic is going on?" I dared to ask.

"We were hoping you would tell us," a male voice answered.

I strained to look in front of me, but where the voice appeared to be, I saw only a spark, and then two more. They flickered in a row of erratic patterns.

"Where am I?" I said obstinately.

"Let's start with the first question, shall we? Answer that, and then we can both move forward."

I closed my mouth and decided to keep it that way.

"She believes she's being smart, brothers," the voice spoke to those who were silent. "Perhaps we should show her otherwise."

I didn't hear a concurrence from whomever the voice was addressing--I only felt a blinding pain shoot through me, almost like when I had touched the door's panel. It disappeared as quickly as it came.

"Now," the voice said smugly, "do you want to be smart or imbecilic?"

I was panting from the shock. I didn't want any more, but I wasn't a fader; my image was true and solid. I couldn't betray the Reuss. And besides, there were worse things than death for faders of the Reuss.

Another shock went through me. This time, I screamed.

"I don't like doing this, especially to those of your quality."

Breathing heavily, I tried stalling. "My quality?"

"Royal. Regal. Wealthy. At least on your insignificant planet."

He knew who I was.

"Daughter of Primum Inash and his mate Emera," he continued, as if reading from a written slate. "You are the youngest to your sister, First Daughter Vorlray, and brother, First Son Emariat. Attended the university in the First Quadrant for two cycles and disappeared for four more. You've only lived for forty cycles, Hmmmm, quite young, served thirty days for thievery, a two-cycle sentence, and then vanished again for another cycle."

I looked forward and noticed that the spark held a steady light as my captor spoke. The other two lights continued to blink. So, there were three of them.

"If you know so much about me," I paused, catching my breath, "then you should already have your answers."

Another shot of pain flung me back. I tensed my muscles to alleviate the pain. It didn't work.

"Wrong answer." He seemed to be enjoying this.

I didn't think I could take any more. My body wasn't fully Wendh; it was much too weak for this.

"Stop!" I whispered, unable to say any more.

"What? What was that, Second Daughter?"

"Please." To talk was unbearable. "Stop."

A surge of strength entered me, which forced me upright.

The second blinking light now held steady, while the first began to blink, as a new male voice asked, "How's that?"

The pain vanished suddenly. That wasn't good. If they could rejuvenate me at will, they could torture me for months. But I had to be strong for the Reuss, for my friends. I had to contain strength.

"Now, perhaps I could help you with your answers." The first voice shifted slightly to the left, and then back to its original position. The steady light moved as well. I assumed he was walking.

He continued. "You have utiq oil on your skin, a techchart in a fleshy fold on your abdomen, and next to that, an inactgun. A false hand-glove is on your left hand, and your eyes are most definitely black, not brown. Have I left anything out?"

"Recheck your data, and you tell me," I answered.

"It's accurate," he said shortly. "Why don't we start with the techchart. Unfortunately, it's already bonded with you. So we can't get the remaining information from it. Perhaps you should access it for us."

Red light fell on my right arm, and it dropped the armrest, releasing me. I thought of the inactgun, but it wouldn't do me any good. He already knew about it, so it was probably disabled. I reached in the skin-pouch and took out the ball, knowing exactly what would happen. Balancing it on my thigh,

I tapped it for the next instructions. The ball shimmered and then spurted dust. Crumbling in my hand, it immediately began to evaporate.

"A pity. Timed out." The second voice held no disappointment. They seemed to have already anticipated the techchart's reaction. "I suppose you'll have to be a story-teller, Jetticia."

He knew my name, though I didn't know why I was so shocked. They knew everything else about me. They had probably taken samples of my DNA and searched my entire history.

Even if I told them everything, I wasn't promised my life. There wasn't anything that would benefit me in this. So I answered, "I lack imagination. Why don't you tell me a story?"

"Tell us what the techchart asked you to do." The second voice ignored my witticism. "We can start there."

I thought of the pain that I knew was still close by, and wondered what part of the story I could tell, which wasn't much. I was only Eyes in this cate, but even Eyes could give out too much detail. I didn't want to begin the construction of a puzzle. I couldn't betray the Reuss. I kept my mouth shut.

"Silence," the first voice said, but I didn't believe he was talking to me. "Very well, let us tell *you* what you were doing here."

"Go ahead," I invited. They couldn't know much.

He inhaled deeply before beginning. "It seems your friends succeeded in their ploy. They kidnapped The Lady of Isdol, and authorities are awaiting their demands."

I laughed. "That's insane. Kidnapping? A high-caste?"

"Believe me, we were just as shocked. Your friends don't seem to have the materials to do such a job. So, someone provided it to them."

I stopped laughing. He was right: the ball, the materials, this type of cate. I knew the devices were too high-tech. The Reuss weren't into kidnapping. Executing, yes, but not kidnapping. Kidnapping was too risky. Was it possible? Would they steal a sentient being? It would explain Vrang's bad attitude.

"We were wondering," said the first voice, "who is your employer?"

"Look at me," I smirked. "If I knew anything, do you think I would be here?"

"Good assessment," the second voice added, "but that does not explain why you were at the front of our door."

Their door?

He waited for an answer, and I knew he wanted one quickly.

"I was sick," I stated bluntly.

"Yes, we saw that."

I paused. Of course. They had been watching me from a viewer. But telling the truth was not my intention. I knew sometimes a little truth gets in the way of fact, but this was not the time.

"But," the first voice inquired, "you seemed to be directed by . . . something."

"Perhaps it was . . . hunger?" I tried to amuse them.

"Really . . . .." The voice lingered on the word. He seemed interested in that piece of information, or at least he thought it was funny.

I was sure my ironic remark would bring about another surge of pain. I braced for it, but there was only silence.

Then the first voice asked, "Have you experienced any lost hours in the past few days?"

"Lost hours? I don't quite understand."

"Missing hours," the voice repeated, "time that you can't account for."

"I could count this as lost time, wouldn't you say?"

More silence.

"Look." I was becoming impatient. It was obvious from their last question that they had nothing to do with Vrang's cate. "Why don't you turn me over to the Enforcers. I'll serve my sentence and you'll never hear from me again. I didn't mean to lean on your little door, okay? It was an accident."

No one answered.

I felt stupid. Perhaps they were stalling before releasing another burst of torture. As soon as I finished that thought, hunger swept in. It had been waiting patiently to re-emerge. I clenched my teeth trying to fight it back. Something was to my right, something that I needed. I needed to go *that way* . . .. *Go that way*.

I looked in that direction, but I could see nothing. The pain leaped several notches, and all I could do was bang my free arm and force my head back to scream.

"What are you doing to her?" It was a new voice, soft and male.

"Nothing," the first voice answered, puzzled.

"I see a battle going on within her," the second voice pompously stated. "She causes her own pain."

"And what does that mean?"

"It means . . . she's dying."

Chapter 4   Examined

I woke up inside a large living creature. Gel substances surrounded me and surged inside my body. I couldn't move, scream, or even breathe on my own; the alien Being did that for me. I could only float in the red gel as it probed every inch of my body, inside and out.

When I awoke next, I was in a small room filled with blazing lights. Smaller bursts of light darted around and shot rays through me sporadically. It burned, and I moaned out loud. I was quickly put back under.

I was narcotized and awakened many times, each time in a new location. Whether they were rays or gels or sonic waves, I realized one thing: I was being studied.

My last awakening was in a brightly lit room with no exits and no walls. I was carefully placed in a long, narrow chair that seemed to sit in a white, empty space. At least this time, my body was no longer in distress, being poked and prodded. I relaxed, closed my eyes and took advantage of the comfort.

"Greetings."

Annoyed, I turned around to see a Hyperian male standing behind me, smiling pleasantly. The many black spikes that surrounded his body poke through a white suit. It made his head look like a swarthy, spiked ball sitting on top of a white tube.

"I have only a few questions, and then I will allow you to return to your sleep." He walked to my side and sat on a lifted stool.

"I wasn't sleeping. I was drugged," I spat. "Now, where am I?"

"You're in good company. I'm here to help you."

I sat up. "I don't need any--. . ." I lay back down and changed my mind. I was still groggy, and my strength was limited. I closed my eyes again, too tired to keep them open. I could answer his questions without looking at him.

"How is your discomfort?" He asked cordially.

I hadn't noticed my pain, but when he mentioned it, I could feel its awaiting presence. Groggily, I answered, "Numbed, but still there."

"Good." The Hyperian said and placed his hand on my thigh, gently massaging it.

I smacked his hand away and jumped up.

"No, no. Please don't be alarmed," he tried to assure me. "I must test something."

"Well, test it on someone else!" I yelled and looked down at myself, seeing that I was covered with a thin gown. I wished I had my inactgun.

"Do you know what I am?" he asked earnestly.

"I know what you are! You're a healing pervert who put me inside the belly of one of the most disgusting creatures of the Four Quadrants to examine me!"

"No, no," he fretted, "I am trying to help."

I found the strength to step towards him. "Keep your 'help' to yourself, Hyperian, or you'll find your spikes littered on this floor!"

A wind filled the room and with it, a familiar voice. "Is there a problem?"

I whipped around and froze. I recognized the being immediately. Who wouldn't? His slick red cowl, with a hood covering only darkness, was known by all, but mostly by the underlings of society. He was Voice, one of the renowned Minions of the Ja'pah.

"Do you need assistance?" Voice questioned, his cloak soundless as he entered the room.

I stared at him, captivated.

"Just a misunderstanding, Maheir Voice," the physician formally addressed him with a bow.

The faceless hood turned in my direction.

I did not move, though my mind was wracked with questions. What was going on? Why was *he* here? Was he the voice that held me captive? *The* Voice?

Voice said nothing as the darkness within the hood surveyed me. The quietness in the room was unnerving, but he soon spoke, turning to leave. "Let me know of your progress."

"Indeed I will," the physician answered promptly and then said to me, "Please seat down. Let us continue."

I did as I was ordered, still staring at the closed door that the Voice had exited.

By the Name! Voice. I didn't know anyone who had ever stood in the presence of the Ja'pah's Minions, and very few ever saw the Ja'pah himself. But there he was: Voice. I felt like I was in the presence of royalty.

"That was Voice!" I whispered to the Hyperian, stunned.

"Yes, I know; now, please hold still," the Hyperian answered.

"What is he doing here?"

"I am only paid to heal you."

"Is he my captor? He's the one who's paying you?"

The physician only remained silent. I couldn't get any satisfactory answers out of him. Either he did not know, or he valued his life too much to reveal what he did know.

He placed his hand back on my thigh, massaging it lightly.

This time I allowed him to continue, though it made me awfully uncomfortable. I tried to think of other things, like Voice.

Voice. His only name. Yet he wasn't quite like the Voice species that lived on my planet and were native to the Wendh's home world, Zendyllic. Voices were hairless and short in stature with wrinkled, soft skin. This Being was tall and slim, and when he lowered his hood, his hair was as red as a flame. He did have the same skin color as the Voice species, the color of dawn. Mostly, he was called Voice because he was the voice of the Ja'pah.

Ja'pah.

Even to think his name sent chills through me. The Ja'pah may have been seeing through his Minions' eyes at that very moment. I could have been in the presence of a sovereign, one who ruled the galaxies equal to Imperial TeNeil. Yet opposite of the Imperial, the Ja'pah commanded and owned all organized crime. He was Imperial to all subordinates; to the Underworld.

I wondered if Voice would return, and if my thoughts were correct regarding his identity. Could he have been the one who interrogated me? And the other two in the room interrogating me--were they the Ja'pah's Minions, Reso and Espy? If so, that explained the many questions, and why I was apprehended shortly after touching the plate on the door. If that was the Minion's room, and I was trying to gain entrance, they must have thought I was an assassin, or perhaps a spy.

"Was he the one who brought me here?" I tried again to get an answer from the Hyperian. "Voice?"

"Please try to concentrate on what I'm doing," the physician said, annoyed with my inquiries.

"You're not doing anything but trying to get me aroused! Now, answer my question!"

He stopped moving his hand. "Is that what you feel?"

That's what I was beginning to feel, but I was too embarrassed and shocked to tell him that.

"Please answer the question," the physician insisted.

"Look, Hyperian. I've already been quenched." At least I *thought* I had satisfied my hunger. "I don't need you irritating it even more."

"Yes, I've seen that. Very recently, in fact, with a Lingar."

I clenched my teeth. This was a very private thing for Wendhs, and he was gawking at it with his mind like rubies on display.

Finally, he removed his hand, turned away and presented me with a small container. "For now, take these every time you feel your need. It may help with the intensity."

I snatched the translucent object containing tablets and looked away, leaning back into the chair. I wasn't getting anywhere with him; however, the medicine was a good sign. I was here to be healed and not killed. Voice could have easily arranged my death, but instead he wished to preserve it. Perhaps the Minions perceived me as unimportant.

Chapter 5   Release and Betrayal

The next thing my eyes lay upon was the inside of my bedroom. Somehow already completely energized, I jumped up from bed and ran around my small apartment, trying to regain my bearings. I had to convince myself that I was actually home again. Once assured, I settled down in the chair in my sitting room and breathed. I *was* home again.

"Bymé," I spoke to my host computer, "What day is it?"

"Two-sixty-six of the Hentpki cycle. Month five, day five of the sixth week," the gentle female voice answered.

Aghast, I asked, "Are you sure?" Before the computer could answer, I said, "Of course you're sure."

"You've been away fifty-four days, exactly one month."

Had it been that long? "How did I arrive back home?"

"You arrived today at the thirteenth hour, asked not to be disturbed, and settled into your resting state."

I didn't remember any of that. It could have happened, but more than likely, Voice had my computer reprogrammed.

"I came home alone, of course."

"Yes."

"By drome?"

"Unknown."

Reprogrammed. I was right. Looking around my room, I didn't see anything amiss, and then panic struck me.

"Bymé, contact Sadotch. Schedule a meeting . . . today."

I had been out of contact with Sadotch since I went to find Vrang. Sadotch had a cate for me after my quench, and I was six weeks late for the briefing.

I put my hand to my forehead, feeling stressed, and noticed something glittering by my head. Looking up, I discovered a bracelet strongly encircled around my wrist. It sparkled with crystals, which were held together with intricate silvery circles of a crystalline compound.

"What's this?"

"A communication device in place of your implanted qCarpus. It is called the Qubit Tachyon, or Qutcy, for short," Bymé answered, though I wasn't talking to her.

"You're in this now? You've been talking to me through this thing the whole time?" I hadn't noticed since I programmed her voice to project at an arm's length distance.

"Yes, Jetta, it is in my programming."

Of course. That was the final proof that Bymé had been tampered with, and also a huge indication of the cost that went into this upgrade.

I looked closely at my wrist, and indeed, my qCarpus was no longer there. One of those physicians must have been paid quite highly to remove it. But why go through all the trouble and the cost? I tried looking for the switch to unchain it, but I couldn't find it.

"Bymé. Where's the latch for this bracelet?"

"You do not have the necessary means for removal."

"What? What do you mean? Are you saying it's like my qCarpus?"

"The qCarpus can be removed by surgical means. This type of device can only be removed by a unique computer structure constructed only for this specific Qutcy. I do not see this device in your dwelling."

What the fleik? "Are you saying I can't take the steic thing off?"

"That is correct."

"Wonderful." Who knew what was programmed on it and what it was meant to do? "So, I suppose you can tell me what this thing does?"

"It does everything that your qCarpus does, but it has twenty times more features. It also contains a techchart as well as an unlimited credit balance."

"Credit balance? What do you mean unlimited? Are you saying it's mine?"

"Unfortunately, Jetta, I have insufficient data on that piece of information."

"If I use this, will the Enforcer come for me?"

"I assume, that because the Qutcy is on your wrist, it is there for your use." Bymé paused slightly. "One moment, please."

I waited as Bymé completed her transaction. It also gave me a little time to brood over the bracelet. Why did Voice place this on me? There had to be more to what Bymé was saying. They must be watching me. But all went well with the cate, according to Voice, and I was sure they knew it was the Reuss who profited from it. The Ja'pah knew everything that went on underground. So why monitor me?

"Jetta," Bymé acknowledged me. "Sadotch will meet you at The Millings in four hours."

Sadotch must have had Bymé notify him when I got back to my quarters, or he had my quarters under surveillance, because the scheduled time for the meeting was entirely too quick. It usually took a few days for me to get a meeting with Sadotch. I stood up, the Qutcy forgotten, and took a breath to prepare for my departure.

# # #

A guard met me at the door, scanned me and let me pass through. I wound my way through the aisles of machinery working on molding and producing organic compounds. The stuff was in high demand this time of year for plants like The Millings. It was in everything I saw around me.

As I continued walking, I looked up and spotted several Beings pacing the railings. I was once one of them, learning to scout and decode every item made from this plant. That was five cycles ago, immediately after I left the university, looking for something else to do with my life. It was Vrang who had broadcast the announcement of new hires for The Millings. I watched it on one of the news pillars on the streets. I took the invitation, not having any other options but to go back home, and stepped through that door, never looking back.

Sadotch provided food, shelter and currency for his employees. It was the ideal place for stragglers. I did not know my work was actually a trade for a thief.

Months later, I joined the Reuss, who worked cates for Sadotch on occasion. My time with them ended with my incarceration. It was my fault, really, not heeding the warning signs; but it was also a chance to get out of the risky cates that the Reuss took on. Cates were escapades for the Reuss, and I wasn't a thrill-seeker. Sadotch came to me right after my release, and I continued to work directly for him. The change of pace was a relief, and the currency was much to my liking.

I pitied those Beings who stealthily walked on the railings as they had been trained. If they had skills like I had, or even a hint of potential, they would be offered the same proposition: join or lose your life. The choice wasn't actually optional.

Then, they would undergo the training. From my squad of fifteen, only three survived. I was second. I counted twenty Beings on those railings, and I knew that I was looking at corpses. Those who did survive would be where I stood now-- looking up at the new breed of thieves.

I kept walking, watching my footing and my surroundings. The Milling was a constant test for alertness. Acuity was essential in this business. One should always be prepared.

I made my way through the maze, dashing by harmless lasers, jumping over sharp objects and squeezing through tight spaces. It was a short obstacle course, if you knew where you were going.

Finally reaching the door, I looked for clues on how to enter. Nothing was ever easy. It took a few moments to find a key and then the lock. I entered into the room, not through the actual door as expected, but through a circular hole above it.

Dropping down into a hallway, all was quiet, but as soon as I walked past the threshold of the next oval door, I heard Sadotch, munching and burping.

The obese worm sat in an enormous chair that floated slightly above the ground. A large table was permanently attached to the chair, never empty of sustenance. Sadotch's appendages, which I considered arms, grew from where his neck would have been had he had one. They were endlessly moving, stuffing his huge mouth with food and swinging back to the table for more.

I strolled into the dimly lit room, watching Sadotch eat. At one time, his constant feeding was distracting; the gulping and belching and incessant chewing made me stutter when I spoke, and it made me squeamish, as well. I learned to remain focused, but I never learned to be inured of it, no matter how many meetings I had with him.

Sadotch was Ayalum, a larva of his species who should have metamorphosed several cycles ago. I believed he enjoyed his present way of life, and to evolve would mean he would have to change the way he lived. Ayalums were feline-eyed, winged, beautiful creatures who passively lived in the Third Quadrant.

Sadotch was too sadistic for that type of life. Or perhaps it was his love for eating that made him remain a larva.

Sadotch chewed before greeting me. "Ahhhh (burp), Jetta."

"Sadotch." I stopped in front of his chair, ready for his questions.

"And where have you been?"

"Indisposed," I answered much more callously than I had intended.

Sadotch chewed on something fleshy, parts of it still hanging out of his mouth. "Not very thorough."

He was indicating my answer. I reported everything to him. It was better to be thorough than misunderstood.

"I had no way to communicate with you until now," I answered. "I came as soon as I could."

He was quiet, which unnerved me. Sadotch usually didn't speak when he was chewing something tasty, but he'd already chewed the same piece of meat for a few minutes.

He gulped, then said, "As we thought. She lies."

I turned to see Tagg walk out of the shadows, twisting his medallion with the royal child imprint. Vrang also appeared by his side. *What was going on? Why were they here?*

Stifling my shock, I said plainly, "I don't lie."

"How do we know?" Sadotch munched. "Wendhs don't lie, we all know that, but you're part of that . . . that other species."

"Human," Vrang cockily aided him.

"Whatever that species is." Sadotch flung more food in his mouth. "How do we know that these Humans don't lie?"

Humans did lie, but I wasn't going to tell them that.

"What is this about, Sadotch?" My nervousness was setting in.

"Like you don't know," Tagg stepped forward, and before I could blink, he shot me.

I was going to see my Goddess at that moment. I knew that before Tagg pulled out his weapon. I thought I saw the flash of light and the wind of souls, but . . . I felt no pain.

A transparent shield swept up in front of me, spurting a burst of light from the Qutcy. On the front was an illuminated, black insignia.

"Ja'pah . . .." Meat fell out of Sadotch's mouth.

Vrang's eyes went round, while Tagg looked at me with utter curiosity.

I took that moment to run.

"Get her!" Sadotch shouted. "We need answers! Don't just -"

I was in the hallway, running back through the obstacle course faster than I had ever gone through it. When I triggered a weapon that shot, I then turned and directing it, before going ahead. The farther I went, the more screaming I heard behind me. Eventually, they would figure out that following directly behind me would do no good; they would have to stop me from ahead. So, I turned back around.

The Mills trained good thieves, and I was one of the best because I used my imagination.

"You're unpredictable," Sadotch had said when I met him for my first briefing on a cate. "That's why I want you on my side."

Unpredictable. That summed it up, for sure, and heading back the way I came was even a new one for me.

I passed Sadotch, who was waiting impatiently for my capture, without stirring him. I headed for one of the numerous exits that were in the room.

Luck was on my side. The exit I chose was one of the short paths. Running a few steps on the sidewall to bypass detection, I hit a transport switch and was jettisoned to an open dirt field outside of the district.

Chapter 6   Home

The message in the streets would spread fast, which meant I was no longer safe on this planet, or this galaxy. I couldn't return to my living quarters, and I didn't know anyone I could trust to hide me. There was only one place I could go.

Home.

Using the Qutcy, I had Bymé signal a drome and used its credit to find me a ship heading for Ytieria. It wasn't easy, because my home planet was so remote. I found a cargo carrier who was flying somewhat close to the vicinity, and I paid a lot of currency from the bracelet for his trouble to divert him briefly from his route. There would be a few detours along the way for cargo drop-offs, but I welcomed the extra days. I needed time to think.

As soon as the ship departed, I went in search for a univice, which I found in an isolated room. I sat in front of the flat surface and asked my first question to Bymé, who linked up with the univice.

"I need to know the latest news of The Lady of Isdol. Start six weeks ago."

The circular device lit up, and a holograph image lit up in its center. There was a scene of a world with a label underneath it, identifying it as Isdol, which zoomed in on a continent, then a city, and then a horde of people crying out in anguish.

"A world distraught. A people traumatized. A leader taken." The disembodied voice, not Bymé's, spoke over the image reported. "The Lady of Isdol has been kidnapped from the Hotel Quitimah this night on the planet Hentpki located in the First

Quadrant. This unlawful seizure happened approximately two minutes ago. Authorities are waiting for the criminals' demands. Who would have thought--"

"Pause," I said, and the image froze. "Skip to the part of the demands."

Bymé replied, "There were no demands recorded for this news."

"Then show me what happened next to The Lady of Isdol."

A new image appeared of a smiling female, her head streamed of green hair that flowed like trillions of fine threads of silk. Her large brown eyes and her white lips were outlined with a green cosmetic that heightened the paleness of her face. She was richly dressed in loose white pants and a matching shirt that hung past her knees.

She was Isdollem, a species that prided itself on being untouched by Wendhs. That wasn't true, of course; many Wendhs had The Calling for an Isdollem, but they were either killed trying to reach the planet, or, if they were able to kidnap their chosen True Mate, they died from the Isdollem, killing themselves by activating a device that they called a Suicide Chip, which was implanted into each of them before puberty.

Wendhs were supposed to mate with other species, never with their own. It was considered quite disgusting, unnatural and blasphemous for Wendhs to do such a thing. A Wendh was to hear The Calling, let it guide them to their mate, and do whatever was necessary to keep their True Mate by their side. And though Wendhs were the dominant species of this part of the universe, there were species like the Isdollem who would kill them on sight if they came too near their planet.

It was the forced mating, the metamorphosis and the kidnapping that made them hate Wendhs. And it was this kind of rejection and persecution that made the Free-Willed, the Wendhs of my home planet, abandon society and begin their own mating rituals. Mating with another Wendh meant no metamorphosis, as Wendhs were already compatible, and it also meant there would be no homesick mates filled with contempt because they were made a slave to a desire that could only be quenched by their True Mate.

So, the Isdollem would rather commit suicide, knowing that a Wendh could not live without his or her True Mate. True Mates were joined physically, mentally and spiritually. A Wendh's True Mate's death meant their own, and the Isdollems were not afraid to take their own life to keep their blood "pure."

The Isdollem were able to get away with their renegade because their planet had an abundance of reoet crystals. These crystals were used to stabilize wormholes, fly ships, make star gates and give energy to an entire planet. One of these crystals had gotten me incarcerated, and had it been on my person, I would have been executed.

I stared at The Lady of Isdol, the ruler of the Isdollems, and thanked Suphyz that Voice had caught me on this last cate with the Reuss, and not the Enforcers. That was twice now that my life had been spared.

"--She's alive!" The exasperated voice of the reporter rose. "The Enforcers were secretly given confidential information by an anonymous Being, and intercepted the thieves' exchange of The Lady of Isdol."

The Lady hugged her brother, Torshincal, and her beautiful cousin, Yolikeg, before vanishing with them into a ship to return to their planet.

"Some of the criminals have been captured," the reporter went on, "but several have escaped. With the interrogation, we hope to find out--"

"Pause," I said, looking around the room to see if I was still alone, and then continued. "Summarize. What happened with the interrogation?"

"The interrogation was never held," Bymé said plainly. "The captured kidnappers were killed during transit to the nearest Enforcer's base."

I sat back in the chair and stared at the frozen image of The Lady, smiling her farewells to an audience of bystanders. Someone betrayed the Reuss, informed the Enforcers where the exchange of The Lady was to be held, murdered those who were caught and devastated the cate.

And they thought the fader was me!

I held my forehead in my hands and shook my head in disbelief. I told the Minions nothing. I didn't even know what the cate was. I was only Eyes, for Suphyz's sake!

Glittering caught my attention, and I looked at the Qutcy. Playing with the light in the room, it was clasped strongly around my wrist as if it dared to cut off my circulation. Staring at it, I pondered what the Ja'pah might have thought. He marked me, forbidding all others to harm me but him; and this thing probably watched my every move.

Why? I was no one, just a petty thief. No, I was a stupid thief who should have noticed Vrang's signs and not given in. Now, the Reuss thinks I'm a fader, Sadotch wants me dead and I'm marked by the Imperial of the Underworld.

Well, at least Sadotch couldn't kill me, but that didn't mean the Ja'pah wouldn't. I didn't know what fate was heading towards me, and I prayed to Suphyz that it wasn't in torment.

"Bymé, show me what happened after the death of the thieves."

The image blinked and then started up again, showing The Lady standing on a podium in front of an audience giving a speech. "We will find who has done this. There will be nowhere to hide for these ruffians!"

Imperial TeNeil's Voice stood up then, adding to the Isdol's plight. "Not only has The Lady been forced to undergo such cruel situations, but the Imperial's cousin, Vortsi, is missing as well. There will be a full investigation, and we will get to the bottom of this. We will--"

"Pause." The image froze, and I stared at the determined faces of The Lady and the Imperial's Voice.

Politics. I hated it and never wanted to be involved in it in the first place. I stood up and Bymé shut off the univice. There was nothing I could do but wait, and I was sure there was some sort of reformatory sentence that I was waiting for.

But was this how it was going to end? This was where my life had led?

I exited the room and moved to the small quarters the cargo carrier had made for me. I needed some sleep.

# # #

It took ten days to get to Ytieria, when normally it would have taken six. We landed in Cavelek, the only place on Ytieria that allowed arrivals and departures of ships. After that, I had to credit a yiplin to ride the rest of the way, as well as some rations. Currency from offworld meant nothing to Ytieria. On my departure from my home world, I had to return with the items given on a list, or else I wouldn't be allowed to leave the planet. Taking note of the items, I knew it wouldn't cost much for my father to provide, but it was a steep price for the average citizen. The animal was the largest mammal on Ytieria and the main source for traveling, so it was one of the most expensive things on the planet.

I had forgotten how yiplins smelled and how it felt to ride in the mounds of folded flesh in the cup of its back. Yiplins had brown and white thin hairs that lay flat against their yellow bodies. Their short necks extended like bellows several feet straight ahead of them, which supported their fast running speed. Not a movement was felt while riding a yiplin. I could never figure out why. I guessed it had something to do with magnetic fields. Its speed was spectacular, but no matter how fast the yiplin ran, it still wasn't fast enough for me. With a drome, I would have been home the same night. It took seven days to reach my father's house by yiplin, which meant no sonic baths, no shelter, no soft bedding, no comfort whatsoever.

I didn't miss the rural life.

It was night when I finally reached the house. That was the perfect time for me, because I didn't want a festive homecoming, something I was sure my father would have wanted to welcome me back home.

The gates were up and inviting. A young Human male ran up to me and took my yiplin's rein. I signaled it to lower for me to dismount and looked at the Human. It had been seven cycles since I had seen a Human. It was almost comforting, reminding me that I was finally home. The boy gawked at my eyes, either realizing exactly who I was or mistaking me for my mother.

"Mistress," he bowed and remained that way when I passed him.

When I was young, I had thought that my father's house was the largest building in the universe. Now that I looked upon it, it seemed quite small compared to the structures offworld. It housed hundreds of Human servants and had numerous rooms. The stone structure was a fortress that rose high in the night sky, but the rock was warm and welcoming.

I entered the courtyard and took in the scent of the many flowers that grew there. The loggia was uncovered, showing the stars above. Balconies circled the walls, which were lined with more flowers. During the day, they would be filled with activity and bodies moving about, but it was late, and no one was outside but a few Ivka guards and the boy who welcomed me by the gate. Pausing for a moment, I made my way to the nearest elevator, or "moving room," as my mother called it, and voiced for the main floor. It was one of the few mechanical things in the house, though my father did have the city of Novarim on his province, where technology was freely used.

I passed a few servants as I made for my room. Their whispering was quite obvious. I didn't mind. They would spread the news of my arrival, and my parents would know by morning. Good. At least tonight I would get some sleep.

Slipping through the door, I went to my four-poster bed and snuggled in the warm blankets, not bothering to change my clothes. It was strange being under blankets again. They felt somewhat heavy when compared to the materials used offworld, but it was comforting. I looked around at my dresser, my full-length mirror, the wardrobe and the closed door to my washroom. The room looked empty compared to my apartment offworld. Such simplicity. Everything had remained untouched. The servants continued to tidy it, I noticed, but everything was where I had left it.

I looked again at the door to the washroom and considered cleaning myself. It had been a long journey, but I was much too tired. I would clean in the morning.

# # #

I awoke with the sunlight burning my eyes. I moved my head back into shadow and looked at the window. It was noon.

Without a smile, I then turned to the Being sitting on the edge of my bed and said, "Hello, Mother."

Emera was silent. Her curled hair was tight around her head. She must have just washed. She was wearing one of my father's favorite gowns. It was red and showed her every curve, and accented her light brown skin. Mother still did things to please my father as if she were still his maidservant, his slave, instead of his True Mate. Only when her eyes burned with coal did she show her feminine strength.

"When's breakfast?" I tried again.

I realized then that I was famished. The dried nuts and meat I had bought for my journey were barely enough to fill my stomach. Plus, I was looking forward to Ytieria's food. It was one of the things that I missed most about home.

My mother's lips were taut, and I could see the tears at the brim of her eyes.

I turned away.

"Not one word," she finally said in a coarse whisper. "One word, in five cycles. We got a message that you were incarcerated, for . . . for stealing--"

"Mother, I don't want to talk about it. I'm hungry." I hugged a pillow. "Can you call a servant or something? I don't have to eat at the table."

"Jetticia . . ." her voice cracked. I knew she was trying to hold her composure.

She sat silently for some time before I felt her weight lift from the bed. She had given up. "I'll send food to your room."

She left as silently as she had come in.

I looked at the closed door and exhaled. Father must not have been home. If he was, he would have been here with my mother, and I wouldn't have been vindicated so easily. But, I wasn't completely spared by my mother, either. She'd regroup her emotions and return, demanding more answers. Until then . . . I would enjoy my native breakfast.

# # #

Mother returned late that day with Primum Inash. Fortunately, my father was just as calm and silent as my mother

. . . at first. He became more determined for answers the more we spoke.

"What was this about stealing reoet crystals? What Beings have you associated yourself with?" His breathing accelerated as I sat silently in the chair of my room.

"You cannot come back here and give us no answers," my mother pleaded. "We just want to help you."

"I don't need any help!" I finally shouted, springing up from my chair. "I just want to be left alone!"

They were stung by my behavior. I had never shouted at them, never said one displeasing word. They stared at me as if I were a stranger.

"I'm sorry," I said. "You don't understand. It's different out there. It changes you. You were the one who wanted me to go," I accused my mother, "not me. I couldn't help what I have become."

They stood silent, not accepting my statement, so I had to appeal to them. I lowered my voice. "I finally came home because . . . because I had nowhere else to go. I need time." I looked into both of their eyes and repeated. "I just need some time."

They looked at each other, probably mentally talking, something I could never hear. Then their face softened as they came to some conclusion.

My father said, "It is good for now that we know you are safe."

"And," my mother added, "that you're away from whatever influences that caused you to change this way."

"Thank you," I said sincerely.

Mother came to me and kissed my forehead, and the Primum gave my shoulder a squeeze. They both exited my room, leaving me alone to think.

But I couldn't think; I could only rest. I had only lain down for perhaps an hour before an annoying child's voice whispered in my ear.

"What are you doing here?"

I slapped at the body, only to hit air as I jumped out of my sleep. Sitting up in bed, I looked to my right to see a Human female child with tight red curls and green, mischievous eyes.

"MOTHER!" I shouted, kicking the blankets off the bed.

"She can't hear you," the impish child teased. "And you can't--"

I threw a pillow out her. "Get out, Tokie! Get out of my room! You're not allowed in here!"

"It's my room now. You left," she said, picking up the pillow and throwing it back at me. "And now you're back, stirring up trouble. Don't you bring trouble to this house, Jetticia! Whatever you did up there, don't bring it down here!"

"MOTHER!" I screamed, jumping out of the bed and storming out of the room.

"Mother!" Tokie mocked, chasing after me.

I turned around in the hallway, pointing my finger at her. "Get away from me, Tokie, or I'll feed you to the Quols."

"The Quols have been extinct for two hundred cycles," Tokie snubbed. "And I'm much too old for children's tales."

"Then you should act your fleiking age!"

"Fleiking, hmph. Well, that's a word I haven't heard in a long time."

"MOTHER!" I shouted again and ran down the halls.

"Jetticia, we use to have so much fun together. Whatever happened?"

I stopped and turned around again. "I grew up. You never did. And we didn't have fun together. *You* had fun! Getting *me* in trouble!"

Tokie shrugged. "It was just play."

I growled, frustrated, and marched down the grand stairs.

"Mother!" Tokie called out. "Mother!"

I covered my ears. The little brat was probably older than this planet, yet she was the most irritating Being I have ever known.

I stopped a servant in the hallway. "Where's my mother?"

"Where's my mother?" Tokie echoed.

I glared at her and turned my attention back to the servant.

He was stunned, probably because he hadn't seen me in cycles. "I . . . I don't know, mistress."

"Then where's my father?"

"In the counsel room, but--" I sped passed him as he shouted, "I don't think you should disturb him!"

I burst into the room, "Father, where's mother--" and then I suddenly wanted to reverse time and heed the servant's words. Primum Inash was in an intense meeting with several Primums of prominent houses.

They all stared at me.

I looked around the room. Glancing behind me, I saw that the little brat wasn't even there.

Inash found his voice, "You all know my youngest, Jetticia. She's been offworld for some time."

Suddenly, I felt out of place as I glanced down at my offworld clothes and my grimy appearance. I hadn't had time to wash. I looked a mess.

The Primums nodded their heads to me, which would have been a perfect opening for me to apologize for my intrusion, but one of them stood up. He walked over to me and took my hand.

"Jetticia. Welcome home. I hope you will be at dinner this evening?"

Dilvaw. He had been pursuing me since my rite of passage. We'd been intimate several times, but I wasn't interested in becoming his mate, which was what he wanted. Unfortunately, my father approved.

"I . . ." I began, and glanced at my father, who gave me a warning look. I had, after all, embarrassed him at this meeting. "I will try," I finally said. "My Inner Soul has been dwindling lately."

Dilvaw smiled and released my hand. "I pray to Suphyz that you will feel well soon."

He bowed to me and took his seat again.

"Father," I said respectfully, "Do you know where mother is? It is of dire importance."

"She's probably in the garden," Inash suggested.

I bowed my thanks and walked backwards out the doors.

After closing them, I growled out loud, only to hear a squeaky voice growl as well.

"Now, that was the most embarrassing thing I've seen in cycles." Tokie appeared with a shimmering light. "And to think I was regretting your coming back here."

I shoved her down to the floor and headed for the garden.

"How rude!" She shrieked before getting up, dusting herself off and trailing me again.

Emera was in the garden as my father had said, but she wasn't alone. Primstress Tranele, my grandmother, was with her. They were very close friends because my mother had saved her life, or so the story goes. The sentenced offender was locked down below and was only let out on the Day of Traitors. It was a day honored especially for him, a day when he was tortured for his treachery on my father and grandfather's house. This male, this Voice Ber Senot, had killed my great-grandfather, and he would have killed my father and grandfather if my mother had not discovered his plot. Before my mother, my grandmother looked at all Humans as simple slaves and servants. Now, she saw my mother as her cohort, her equal.

"Jetticia! Tranele held out her arms.

"Grandmother." I went to her, slightly uncomfortable as she encircled me with her determined arms.

She was a stern female, even stoic most of her life, with extraordinary dignity. Mother must have already explained what she could of my situation, and I was sure I would hear something from the PrimstressPrimstress's mouth.

"You've lost weight." Tranele looked at me disapprovingly. "And your hair is a mess. And you haven't bathed."

I removed myself from her arms and glanced uneasily at my mother.

"No, she hasn't bathed," Tokie chimed in, "and she interrupted Primum Inash's meeting with such rude behavior that--"

"Mother," I hissed. "Tokie."

Emera held her hand out to Tokie, and the redheaded girl went to her gleefully. "Bothering my daughter again, I see."

"Like she never left," Tokie beamed.

"Mother," I pleaded, "I really have a lot on my mind."

"Huh!" My grandmother said, recoiling. "Young Beings don't know anything about strenuous life."

My mother smiled.

I disagreed, but I was no match in a debate against my grandmother, so I kept my mouth shut.

"I know what you're thinking," Tranele said, her eyes intent on mine. "Offworld is much more complicated than on Ytieria, but, young one, it is only as complicated as you make it. There are choices; there are always choices."

So, that was that. She had said her peace. I was let off quite easily. She stood up. "Your mother and I were discussing going to Ostinia."

My grandmother rarely asked anyone anything. Most of her questions sounded like statements instead. "My Inner Soul has been dwindling," I repeated, declining my grandmother's offer. "How long will you be staying? And where's grandfather?"

"Home, of course," the Primstress answered. "I came to offer my services for Emariat's birth anniversary."

"Birthday . . .?" I was stunned. I had forgotten such things.

"In two days," my mother explained. "He and his mate--"

"Mate?"

"Yes, his mate, Jetticia," Tranele frowned. "You have been gone for some time, you know."

"Yes . . . of course," I stammered, feeling annoyingly embarrassed. I didn't want to go to town with them, and I didn't have a gift to give. *How could I go to the festivities at all?*

And Emariat has a mate . . .

"Emariat and his mate will be arriving for tonight's dinner. We should be going," The Primstress said. "We will see you later tonight." Without another word, she turned her back and headed for the stables.

Mother gave me a kiss, grabbed Tokie's hand and left as well. Their sudden departure poked a fiery hole in my heart. They acted as if I had been gone only a month. Serves me right, of course. They would not detour their lives merely because I happened to arrive unannounced. If my decisions did not hold them in high regard, then they, in turn, would treat me the same way.

Tokie turned around and stuck her tongue out at me. It was a Human, offending gesture, something that shouldn't have bothered me, but it did. I returned the favor, a childish way to behave, I knew, but I couldn't think of any other recourse. I watched them until they turned the corner and then decided I needed to find someone who could give me advice.

# # #

Sage Yamar lived mostly in the twisting tunnels beneath Primum Inash's house. He only came out on rare occasions or for festivals like the one the house was hosting in two days. He was my mentor, second father and my friend. I had gone to him since I was a child, daring even then to find the Sage's quarters and peek through the door at the mysterious silver-headed Wendh. It had been cycles since I had seen him, since I had made my way through the maze underground, but eventually I found my way.

He was sitting, as usual, at a large desk covered with translucent glass flasks containing unknown substances. Yamar was constantly dabbling with this or that, experimenting with things he would never explain to me.

"What's that?" I always used to ask him, though as I grew, my questions had become just a game.

"Ssssomething you wouldn't underssstand," he would always answer.

That was how I approached him now.

"What's that?"

The Sage spun around in his chair, his silver hair and silver eyes sparkling for a moment before he recognized who was standing at his door. He was old, very old, being that he had come with the first settlers of Ytieria, more than four hundred cycles ago, and still he lived. He was the only Wendh with eyes that were not black, at least visibly. The true color of a Wendh's eyes are shielded behind darkness.

He smiled, his sharp teeth bright against his black skin, as he answered fondly, "Ssssomething you wouldn't underssssstand."

"Oh, I think I would understand now, Sage." I replied, stepping into his room and closing the door after me.

"No, no, young one. Not even now."

I found a chair covered with books and paper, cleaned it off, and pulled it up in front of him. He placed his hand on my cheek and gave me a smile--the first warm welcome I had received.

"Hard life, young one. Not neccccccesssssary."

I placed my hand on his. "It was at the time."

His features contorted as if he tasted something bitter, and he removed his hand from my cheek. "Ssstealing reoet crystalsss. In league with thievesss that call themsssselves Reuss. Very ssskilled and mythical group, never been caught, or ssseen, but heard of everywhere."

He knew of the Reuss, and even the name! That wasn't in my arrest record, I knew, which told me he knew about the Underworld. I wondered what other secrets this old one held.

I turned my face away from his disapproving eyes. "They didn't find the crystals on me, Yamar. It was only by suspicion that I was apprehended."

"Enough for a sssentence," he said disapprovingly. "You were carelesssss."

I stifled a smile. It wasn't that I had stolen that angered him; it was that I had gotten caught. He reminded me why I loved him so much.

"You have sssomething on your mind," he said, picking up my wrist and examining my Qutcy. "Very interesssting. Very expensssive. Very high-tech."

"She's called Bymé," I said proudly. "I've programmed her with a unique personality."

"Really."

I nodded. "Bymé, greet Sage Yamar."

"Greetings," Bymé said, her voice sounding strange to me in these familiar surroundings.

The Sage straightened up for a moment. "Interesting."

"She can't do much here. There isn't any technology for her to tap into," I explained.

Yamar nodded his understanding, and I knew he comprehended more than he was showing. In the past, I had suspicions that the Sage left Ytieria from time to time, going offworld to travel between the stars. That was my childish reasoning when weeks and sometimes months went by and he was not below in the tunnels when I went to search for him. The way he looked at my Qutcy and his lack of questions about it made me believe that my childhood hunches were right.

"I am marked, Sage Yamar," I bluntly stated, changing the subject. "I am hunted." The tears filled my eyes, but I did not let them fall.

"Then you mussst face your enemiesss," he whispered plainly. "Find them and do it quickly. Either way, you will die."

I let the tears fall then, knowing what he spoke was true. I wiped at them and changed the subject. "Emariat will have festivities in two days. I will leave after that."

Yamar shook his head sadly, his silver eyes glistening. "No. You mussst leave now. The longer you ssstay here, the more at risssk you placcce your family. Go now. Handle your fate and try to dessstroy your enemiesss."

I wanted to protest: I had just arrived! How could he send me away already? But when I looked into his eyes, I saw his pity and his wisdom. Again he spoke true, and I knew I had to obey. "I will leave tonight."

He turned away from me, returning back to his table of mysteries, and I wiped more tears from my face. As I made my way to the door, the Sage's voice floated to my ears. "Come back sssafely."

The Sage was always contradictory. First, he said I would die, and in the next breath, he asked me to return safely. But long ago, I learned that he spoke of both sides of a truth, a choice. Which one I chose was always up to me. He simply spoke to me of both choices.

# # #

I finally bathed later that night and prepared a sack of food to eat. Primstress Tranele and Emera had already returned and insisted that I come down for dinner, but I gave them no answer. They would learn much later that I had gone. Looking around my room, I made sure everything was in order, and then picked up a royal ring with my father's insignia as proof of my bloodline. I would have the seller charge my rent of the yiplin to my father's credit. Before leaving the room, my eyes fell back to my dresser to see a barrette, possibly placed there by my mother. It was one of my favorites when I was younger. Grabbing it, I pulled my hair back and clasped it in my hair. I took the servants' halls down to the stables, found my yiplin and headed back to Cavelek.

I didn't believe anyone would pursue me. They would allow me to find my own way in life without interfering. I cried every night until I arrived at Cavelek, knowing that once I left Ytieria, I would not have much time to cry again. My mind had to be totally in sync with my agenda--finding the Ja'pah.

Chapter 7   Hilarious Calling

Trying to locate the Ja'pah wasn't easy. My first method was to use as much of the credit in my Qutcy as possible, and then do a trace to find out who was paying the bills. I came up empty. My second step was to locate the doctor who provided my prescriptions and possibly the others who had tested me, but that was to no avail, either--the doctors were unknown and the prescriptions were unlimited, just like my credit.

During my search, I stayed away from territories that might have been covered by the Reuss or by Sadotch's employees. I had no friends, though many, when paid enough, aided me with valuable information for my search. Yet everything led to a dead end, and soon I ran out of ideas and leads. To make things worse, I began to feel my hunger increasing again, as I was no longer adhering to the medication, and the males that I found with healthy physical credentials whom I took to my bed didn't suffice.

I found a hotel somewhere on an unpopular planet in the First Quadrant and settled in, trying to figure out what to do next, when the first wave of overwhelming pain hit me. I doubled over on the floor, my sight temporarily blinded with the agony.

"What's this I see?" a familiar voice teased.

I adjusted my eyes at the shimmering light in front of me, and when it dissipated, there she stood in her perfect dress, with her familiar red curly hair and toothy grin.

"Tokie!" I spat, grabbing the edge of a chair and pulling myself up. "What the fleik are you doing here?"

"I've been here all along," she said, skipping around the room. "Nice hotel. Much better than the last one we stayed in."

Another pain shot through me, and I muffled a moan. I had to sit down.

"Pretty bad, huh?" Tokie walked towards me, but didn't come too close. "And you haven't figured out yet what's ailing you. I thought you were much smarter than this."

I clenched my teeth. "What are you talking about?"

"Your pain, of course. I know what it is, you know."

I rolled my eyes and closed them. Maybe when I opened them, she would be gone.

"Don't you want to know what it is?" Tokie teased. "It's very simple. I'll give you a hint. Your mother had it, and it was pretty bad for her--"

I ran forward, picked her up by her forearms and thrust her against the wall. "I don't have time for this, Tokie! Spit it out!" I shook her and slammed her into the wall again.

And then it started. Her lips began to quiver, and her eyes glossed over with tears.

"Don't you do it, Tokie," I threatened. "Don't you cry!"

But it didn't discourage her as her mouth opened wide, showing me the depths of her throat.

"Tokie!"

She inhaled, sucking in as much air as her lungs could muster.

"I'm warning you!" Before I could think of another threat, she paused and then waaaaaaiiiiled.

The sound stabbed my eardrums like launched spears, and I dropped her to cover my ears from the sound.

"Tokie!" I screamed, but I couldn't even hear my own voice over her screeching torment.

With hands still cupped around my ears, I passed through the glistening field of the doorway to the bedroom, and the horrific sound was almost muted. I could still hear her shrill voice, even through field of the high-tech door, and I knew it would continue for hours.

I paced the floor, my pain suddenly forgotten and replaced by steel rage. "I'm not going to apologize to her. I'm not going to do it."

I fell on the bed and pulled the corners of it to release the soft material that automatically covered me. I yanked more to cover my head, but I could still hear her. Convincing myself that I had a long day and that I could easily go to sleep, I closed my eyes and waited for bliss, but the small sounds of Tokie's screams continued to float in through the door.

Sleep would not come easily. In fact, it didn't come at all. Utterly annoyed, I flung the bedding off and stormed back into the living quarters, making sure I covered my ears. Tokie's screams were as strong as the first sounds that had wailed through her throat. Her face had turned completely red, and her preened dress was drenched, as if she had just splashed through a puddle of water.

"You're going home tomorrow, Tokie," I tried to distract her, but her crying continued. "If you don't stop crying, you're going home tonight!"

The screaming continued.

I tried to soothe her. "You want something to eat?"

That only made her scream louder.

"Ti'senot." I tried dismissing her and stormed back out of the room, but all I could do was pace. I turned back around and decided to confront her. "You're much too old to be acting like this, Tokie! I'm in a dilemma here. I don't need this!"

Nothing worked. I stared at her, slumped on the floor, her mouth wide open, her strident cries filling every space in the room.

I knew the only thing to make her stop crying was to give in. I gave in. "Steic, Tokie," I whispered through clenched teeth. "I'm sorry."

Silence. Even through her piercing cries, she heard my soft apology. The echo of her screams dissipated as Tokie closed her mouth. She stood up and pointed her small finger at me, her hair no longer perfectly curled, her eyes burning emerald fire. "Don't you *ever* do that again!"

Her voice had changed to that rare tone of a mature female. I have only heard her use that voice perhaps four times in my life. She only used it when she felt it was important, and this time she used it as a threat. She did look quite demonic with her eyes glowing green and her hair and face bright red. I was taken aback for just a moment, but I quickly got over her mendacious act and stepped forward.

"Go home."

Our eyes locked in a blazing fury, until Tokie folded her arms and simply said, "No." Her eyes turned back to their normal green, and her face again became a placid, calm white.

I stared at her stubborn stance and then doubled over again in pain. I should have known that it hadn't gone away. As the wave of pain decreased, I looked back up at Tokie without saying a word.

Something changed in her, something that looked like pity, and she sat down on the floor beside me. "You need to go where the pain is less. Point to the direction, and we should go there."

At first I didn't understand what she was saying, but when the pain hit again, I stood up and walked out of our room and kept walking until we were far from the hotel. Tokie trailed behind me at a safe distance, knowing if she came too close I would probably maul her. I walked in the direction where the pain seemed less tormenting, and this continued for hours until I stopped, exhausted.

Slumping to the ground, I rubbed my tired eyes. "It's eased up some, but it's still there."

"Then we're going the wrong direction," Tokie insisted. "We may need to go *up* in that direction. Call a drome and take us to a terminal."

I did what she said, too weary to argue and too drained to demand specifics of what she knew.

I allowed Tokie to handle everything. She spoke at the terminal when we arrived, asked the flight agent which ships were heading in the direction of the Urlanshoran Star that was in the Fourth Quadrant and the farthest destination, and what occupied planets were along the way. The farther a ship had to go, the more stops it had to make. She chose a path and a ship that pleased her. I was too sick to focus on the particulars, and simply held up my wrist to make the Qutcy available to pay for the travel. Within the hour, we were on our way, and the pain began to gradually subside.

# # #

I woke up feeling groggy, trying to remember the previous night's events. I felt as if I had worn a narcotic patch for three days. I sat up, noticing I was sleeping on the floor next to the bed. Dragging myself to my knees, I looked around at a lavish room that made me think I was in a mansion. The room had an atmospheric sensation that allowed clean air to circulate, giving it a fresh, even dainty feeling. Silk cloths hung down from the ceiling, blowing gently with the wind, which added to the effect.

I saw Tokie sleeping angelically in a bed with a blissful smile on her face. While I slept on the floor, she was cushioned in piles of fluffed pillows.

I pulled one of her curls.

"Ouch!" Tokie sprung up. "That hurt!"

"Where are we?" I demanded.

"Jancso," Tokie answered, rubbing her head. "It's in the Third Quadrant."

"Third Quadrant! What in Suphyz name. . ... How did we get here?"

"Jetticia--" Tokie tried to soothe me.

"It's Jetta. That's what I'm called out here."

"Jetticia," Tokie smiled, stretching her arms up in the air, "don't be silly."

I grumbled. Getting a straight answer out of Tokie was like jumping into quicksand and trying to swim out. "Just answer the question. What kind of ship did we take? How many days?"

Tokie actually gave in. "Just two days. Don't worry, you paid for it." She stood up and stretched some more. "We had to take the best; it was urgent."

"Urgent! It wasn't *that* urgent."

"Your pain is gone, isn't it?" Tokie tilted her head in her pseudo-innocent way. "We stopped at two other planets before this one, and it didn't go away, but now it has. So, let's get ready to meet him."

I shook my head, confused. "What are you talking about? Meet who?"

Tokie rolled her eyes. "Do I have to explain everything?"

I looked at her.

"You shouldn't threaten me, you know," the little imp wagged her finger at me. "I saved your life. You should be thankful."

I pulled myself up onto the bed, my head warning of a headache. "Get to the point, Tokie."

"Your mother was much more appreciative when I saved her. She--"

"I'm out of here." I jumped up and left the room.

"Wait!" Tokie ran after me, pleading. "By the Name, Jetticia."

I turned and gave her a look.

"Jetta. I'm just trying to help."

"Then help someone else." I looked around the hotel's living room and knew that this room probably cost more than my father's house and one of his towns. I wanted the Ja'pah to come out of hiding, but I didn't want him to kill me for insolvent credit.

"Pretty nice, huh," Tokie said behind me. "I haven't seen such beauty in quite some time."

"It will probably be your last time," I mumbled, staring at the beautiful table and the floating globes of light. "And my last, too."

Tokie cocked her head. "What was that? I didn't hear you."

"Ti'senot," I dismissed her question. "We have to get out of here."

"I haven't washed yet," she pouted.

"We'll wash later."

"But you can't go to your mate looking like that," she gave me a disgusted look.

"My what--?"

"I guess I *do* have to explain everything," she snubbed, but before I could snap at her, she said very quickly, "Your True Mate is somewhere on this planet because your pain ceased when we got here, and it's the only indication that we came to the right place, and please don't threaten me because it's getting pretty annoying."

I made a sound that voiced the many thoughts that jumbled through my mind. Mate? Pain? *She's* Annoyed?

I paused to sort through the questions and chose the most important one. "Are you saying that--"

"You're in Calling." She smiled as she saw my reaction. "You're not fully Wendh, you know. Don't have the mental abilities. How else will Suphyz let you know that you need to go to your True Mate? You can't hear Her song, thus the pain. It's the only thing that would get your attention. She did the same thing to your mother, too. Made her see that your father was the one she was chosen to be with."

For a moment I was stunned, but it passed quickly as a burst of laughter surprisingly jumped out from what felt like the dusty depths of my being. "The Calling? Are you insane? That's the most ridiculous thing I have ever heard." Yet my laughter grew stronger, making me forget our dilemma. I laughed until my stomach hurt, and I laughed more when I saw the vexed expression on her face.

"That's what it is," she scowled. "Your mate is here."

I fell on the floor.

"It's not that funny."

I howled, releasing all of the tension I had been suffering from for so long.

"Jetticia. It's not that funny."

I laughed more until I became light-headed. Remembering that our lives were on the line, I tried to gather myself together. "We have to go," I said between gasps of breath. "But then again, I think I would rather die from laughing than from the Ja'pah's vengeful fury."

Tokie stormed out of the room, and I followed, still laughing.

# # #

I sat Tokie down in the lobby and told her to stay as I went to the front desk to settle the bill. It was an old-fashioned way to do things, but the management at this hotel obviously thought it gave them more cachet. If I had remembered to check out with using Bymé in the room, I wouldn't have had to do it the inconvenient way. It took longer than I expected, because I didn't know Tokie had ordered several items to be shipped to our room for the next few days for "our" leisure. The hotel charged for the cancellations, and even more for the short notice. After paying the total, I turned around to look for Tokie, my mind steaming, when my heart stopped.

She was there, grinning and ranting like most little girls do when they have someone's attention, but the Being who was being so attentive was. . . Voice. Standing next to him was his brother, Reso, cloaked in blue.

I should have run and left Tokie to fend for herself. After all, she did come along without permission. But I knew that they knew I was already there.

Looking around, I could see the hotel's guests whispering and indicating the two Minions in the lobby. I shared their slight fear. The Minions couldn't murder me in this lobby; at least I didn't think so, though there were ways to prolong someone's killing by pricking them with a poison that wouldn't go into effect until hours later. I didn't think I had been pricked.

"Jetticia. Over here." Tokie waved her hands at me, and my first thought was that I was glad she was going to be murdered along with me. My second thought was that I knew I had no escape, and I might as well get it over with. *Would Suphyz welcome me in Her arms? Have I really done so much evil?*

Slowly, I walked towards them.

"Ahhhh, Jetta," the Ja'pah's Voice Minion greeted me, his red cloak glistening slightly in the mild hotel light. "I didn't fathom seeing you here."

I bet. I took Tokie's hand and pulled her beside me. "Tokie, you choose such strange company to bother."

"She wasn't a bother at all." Voice's smile was the only visible part of him, as the rest remained hidden under the shadow of his hood. "She has such a way of telling stories."

"Stories that I have never heard before," Reso added. His voice was soft and soothing. He wasn't known to speak too often, as he was usually seen standing in solemn silence. His facial features were completely hidden in the darkness of his hood. No one had ever seen his face, nor the third Minion's, Espy, whose cloak was green. The three of them seemed to be just as anonymous as their Ja'pah.

Voice, however, enjoyed showing his face, as his features were admired by several female species. He unveiled himself even now, allowing his red, flaming hair to stream out over his shoulders as he lowered his hood. "My brother and I were just going to our resting quarters, and afterwards we were going to dine. Perhaps you and your little kin would join us?"

Tokie beamed. "Sure--"

"We don't have time," I said, grabbing her closer. "There are a lot of sights that I promised my charge I would show her. Perhaps some other time."

Voice continued to smile, searching my eyes for some weakness. "Then we insist that you dine with us later tonight." He held out a small device that glittered and looked like a gem. "We will be there. Do not disappoint us." There was an edge of warning in his tone.

Tokie grabbed the invitation device, stuck it on back of her hand and aimed her brightest smile at Voice. I glared at her and tugged her to the exit before saying another word.

"I hope to see you again," Tokie shouted over her shoulder, before the doors silently slid behind us.

I couldn't speak. My only thought was to put as much distance between the hotel and ourselves as we could, and to kill Tokie somewhere in between.

As we walked outside in silence, Tokie began to whine about showering again and how her stomach was going to implode from the lack of food. I found a rest stop to attend to her needs. We bathed in the public cleaning facility and found a small table in the dining area to eat. Bymé took our orders and when the food came, surprisingly I also ate, not realizing my tremendous appetite equaled Tokie's.

"You haven't spoken to me since we left the hotel," Tokie said as she stuffed her mouth. "We should have eaten there. I ordered--"

"You ordered our deaths!" I hissed at her, and then I was suddenly conscious of the crowd around us. I hit the button in the middle of the table for privacy. A translucent field surrounded us, and I bent closer to Tokie despite our sequestered shielding. "You knew who you were speaking to. You allowed yourself to get caught!"

"I wasn't caught," Tokie sneered back. "You were caught. They had just entered the hotel, obviously to see you."

"If it weren't for you, they wouldn't have found me!"

Tokie leaned towards my face. "You were looking for them anyway."

"I wanted to find *them*, not the other way around!"

"What difference does it make?" Tokie sat back in her chair and pointed to my Qutcy. "They knew where you were all the time anyway. But they should be the least of your problems. You have to find your mate, and the longer you linger, the closer you get to death."

"This is not a game, Tokie!"

She changed her voice. "I'm not playing one." Her eyes flashed green, no longer displaying a hint of mirth.

I sat still and considered her altered mood. "You're serious."

"Very," she replied in a wise, competent woman's voice.

"You think my hunger is--"

"Yes."

"That we came to this planet because--"

"Yes."

Leaning back, I chuckled, "That's totally ridiculous."

Tokie shrugged, her voice mutated back to its impious tone. "I speak true. Believe me or not. But if you do not find him, it won't be the Ja'pah's Minions who would be your death. But, if you do find him, you'll increase in power and will at least have a chance at whatever you plan to do when you find the Ja'pah."

Snickering, I asked, "And if I did consider finding this True Mate of mine, how would I go about doing it?"

"You follow your hunger, like I've been telling you."

I thought of rejecting her, telling her that it wasn't there anymore, but when I turned my mind inward, I could still feel it lurking, waiting to torment me with its presence.

"Jancso is a very pretty planet," Tokie said, slamming her small hand on the table's button. Immediately, the murmuring sounds of the crowd filled the space around our table. "We should take in the sights while we're here." Tokie jumped up after stuffing the last piece of food into her mouth. "We have a few rays before the moons show themselves."

"We're not touring--"

"Come on, Jetticia, let me show you Jancso. It's been dozens and dozens of cycles since I've been here. Did you know it's Isdol's rival for the reoet crystals? It doesn't produce nearly as much as Isdol, but it can produce some amount."

Tokie grabbed my wrist and yanked me out of the rest stop. "Look! Look at the beauty! Just a few of the crystals on this planet makes Jancso this rich."

I snatched my hand from hers and folded my arms. "We don't have time for this." But I looked up anyway.

Colorful streamers filled the air, and multicolored tunnels flickered between the buildings. Beings smiled and nodded to each other as they passed, and the dromes seemed to display the same courtesy. The buildings themselves moved around in constant flux, as if in a dance. It looked as if the planet was one huge festival. This world was like none I had ever seen. The colors even seemed jubilant and alive, and I wondered why I didn't notice it when we first walked out of the hotel, but then again, I did know why.

I cut my eyes at the painted scene when I glimpsed Tokie grinning at me. "Ti'senot."

"Ti'senot?" Tokie exclaimed. "You can't dismiss this. This place is beautiful, and you agree. You admitted it in your eyes." She twirled around. "It's one of the most beautiful planets I have ever seen. It's in the top list of about twenty planets that I admire. It's kept itself up quite well."

"When did you say the last time you were here?"

"A long time ago." Tokie waved her hand as if to swipe the question aside. She never would admit to her age. "Come. We need to search for your mate. Which way?"

I wanted to turn away from her and leave her there, but I couldn't think of a reason to do it. My mother would never forgive me.

"You should go home," I concluded. "Mother will be worried. We're heading for the terminals."

"No!" Tokie began to pout. "I'm not going home. There's a good story here. A very good story. I knew it involved one of Emera's children, but I didn't think it would be you. I'm stuck here with you, and I don't like it any more than you do, but the story is more important than your rude behavior."

"Story! You're not following me around like you followed my mother, Tokie. You're not going to pester me--"

"I'm here to stay! I already left a note with your mother. And besides, someone had to finally look after you. You make a mess of things too much."

Ignoring her insult, I shook my head in confusion. "What do you mean you already left a note? How did you follow me anyway?"

Tokie grinned, twisted her waist to and fro and pointed to her head. "I cleared off most of the junk on your dresser. I knew you would wear me."

I gasped. "The barrette! You were in my hair! The entire time!"

"As I said, someone has to look after you, and I'm a slave to the story." She laughed as she looked around. "And it's turning out to be quite an interesting one."

I grabbed her by the back of her neck and yanked her to my side. "You're going home." I raised my Qutcy to my mouth. "Bymé, give me directions to the terminal."

"I'm not going back!" Tokie screamed, but her public display wouldn't embarrass me this time.

I watched as a holographic image sprouted up in front of my eyes, displaying my location and the destination of the terminals. Then Bymé signaled a drome.

# # #

The terminals were on the other side of the world, but the drome didn't make it even a third of the way before the hunger pains made their roaring entrance. I tried not to succumb to them and make myself believe that I could see Tokie off in a ship back to my home world, but it overwhelmed me and I was on my back within the hour, my knees pulled up to my chest.

"Don't worry." Tokie began to shimmer, and soon a tall Trecian male stood over me with green flaky skin, bulging muscles, green eyes and short, spiked red hair. "Bymé, turn drome around," he throated.

I submitted myself to Tokie's care again. She paid for the drome and found some new lodgings, not as expensive as the first hotel, but close. The hunger subsided, and I lay in the bed trying to regain my strength.

It was night when I recovered, this time fully aware of the hunger lingering close behind. I got up and looked around the rented room, finding no one there. Soon, the Trecian male entered, carrying a large plate of desserts. He grinned at me before stuffing something white and creamy in his mouth and shimmering. Tokie changed back to her childlike self and grabbed more sweets from the plate. "Delicious."

I didn't have a response.

"You should try some. I know you're . . . hungry," she teased.

I didn't find it funny.

"Where's your sense of humor, Jetticia?"

"Jetta."

"Ti'senot," she mocked me with a smile, and then quickly changed the subject. "Believe me, now, do you? Admit it. You can't leave Jancso without fulfilling the destiny that Suphyz has intended for you."

I folded my arms. I wasn't about to agree.

"And you need me. See? I've saved your ungrateful bottom twice now."

"And endangered it as well."

She pointed her finger at me. "No, you did that."

I walked out.

She followed. "If you don't listen to The Calling, you're going to die."

I grabbed her wrist, gave her an exaggerated smile and plucked the gem from the back of her hand. "I already have a date with death, remember?" I waved the invitation device in front of her eyes. "I can't get off this planet, so the obvious thing to conclude is that those Minions have something to do with my pains. I'm going to find out what they did to me."

"I'm coming, too. I can help."

"You're staying here."

"I'm going with you!"

I left the room without her, and when I reached the hotel exit and turned around, she wasn't anywhere around. I activated the invitation device and signaled a drome to fly me to the invitation's programmed destination.

# # #

What I thought would be an elegant restaurant turned out to be a night establishment filled with performers, dancing natives, lights and music. Food hung down from the ceiling and chairs floated in the air. One would only have to hop on a seat to be delivered to the tasty morsels hanging on velvet strips of rope. The club was exclusive, and if I didn't have the gem, I wouldn't have been allowed entrance. But the gem also had me escorted away from the public by two of the club's guards, up two flights of stairs to a private balcony.

Voice was sitting in a tall-backed chair between Reso and Espy. It was rare to have two Minions in one place, but even rarer to have all three. As soon as I was shown a chair, I felt my hunger jerk. There was something here that urged me, something I wanted desperately. I stifled the need.

"I'm glad you were able to join us," Voice's red hood nodded to me. "Where is our little friend?"

I thought of saying she wasn't able to make it, but instead, I said, "This isn't the sort of place someone so young should see."

"True, very true." Voice bent forward and picked up a small cup. "Deluxar wine. Quite tasty. That space station makes only the finest. You should try some."

I glanced at the filled cup in front of me and wondered what kind of poison could possibly be inside it. Then again, poison could have been on the arms of my chair, seeping into my skin as I sat. I lifted my arms. "I'll pass."

"Of course," he took a sip. "You would like to get on with business, I suppose."

I remained silent. "The business" was my death, I assumed, but I didn't believe it was the reason the Ja'pah's Minions invited me here. They could have killed me any time--had an assassin visit me at my home, at the hotel, in transit, anywhere. There was something else that they wanted, or at least something they thought I could provide for them.

Voice pulled back his hood. I had to admit, his features were quite attractive. His dark brown eyes filled his entire sockets, with black eyelids accentuating them. He wore his red hair like a ruby encrusted crown, drawn back from his perfectly shaped ears, and his skin was unflawed with that beautiful color of the first light of day.

"You have us quite . . . flabbergasted, Jetticia."

"Jetta," I corrected.

He bowed his acceptance. "Jetta. We are still fumbling over the precision of your tracking."

I sat still, baffled. "Tracking?"

"Come now," Voice showed his even-grown teeth, with two upper teeth sharpened at the tips. "Let's not play games. We wouldn't want to have to repeat our first encounter. It's so unnecessary."

I gritted my teeth at his threat.

"So," he said, placing his cup back on the table, "how did you find our location so . . . directly and rectilinearly."

They knew I was looking for them, but-- "It's just a coincidence."

"Coincidence," Reso voiced softly, but said nothing more.

"Not an accident," Voice said, his lips moving as he continued to taste the wine. "Not lacking many flaws. We plotted your route, Jetta. There was no mistaking your path. Every stop that we made, you made. You followed us with precision."

"I don't know," I admitted, my mind filled with confusion.

With that, Espy stood up. "I see no faltering, and I don't see any modification."

Reso stood as well, and the door opened.

"Have a pleasant night," Voice stood, bowed in my direction and walked out after his brothers.

Was that it? That's all? I sat there dumbfounded for several minutes. Something must be wrong. Espy, whose Minion eyesight could see through anything, probably looked at my biology and saw that I was not lying. But what modification was he talking about? And why leave so suddenly? I looked at my arms and checked to see if I felt any nausea. They must have poisoned me. Some kind of poison that would go on for days, or maybe weeks, and the pain was its warning signs.

I walked out of the room, my mind in a fog. The moment I entered the public arena, a Trecian male approached me with a demanding grunt. "Dance with Birken."

I declined politely. "I've had enough festivities for tonight, but thank you."

The male's green eyes flashed before he walked away, and I frowned. I didn't hesitate to leave the club and head back to the hotel. I assumed Tokie would stay and dance for the rest of the night; she enjoyed parties. That was good, because I didn't want her to see me die.

I waited for death for the rest of the night before the hunger presented itself again. The Trecian male returned in the morning, just in time to see me writhing in pain. Tokie took charge and arranged for our departure, choosing the flight to our next destination based on my weak pointing. She was an invaluable help, I had to admit, and I began to think that she might have a point about my hunger pangs. Could I actually be in Calling?

Chapter 8　Meteoroids

This planet was Quuto, located in the Second Quadrant. It took five days to reach it, but my pain only lasted for two of them. I should have enjoyed the rest of the travel because the destination was not as gratifying.

Unlike Jancso, Quuto was mostly dark, its sunrays waned, and its nights were longer than the daylight hours. All this made for an unfriendly place, filled with vile criminals. It made the Renavid district look like Suphyz's paradise.

"Why would your mate want to come to unlawful grounds?" Tokie drilled me, looking around the terminal with dim lights and menacing Beings. "But, I guess you are what you mate."

I withheld my disdain, concentrating on the matter at hand. I still wasn't sure if this was the answer, but it was tangible for now.

"I can't believe you think he's here. He sure jumps around a lot, doesn't he?" she continued. She waved me in front of her and said, "Point the way."

We pushed through the unfriendly crowd. I believe the only reason no one challenged us was that we were still in the terminal. For a moment, I wanted to stay right there. Once we stepped outside in the darkness, the air seemed to pulse with violence.

"Stay close to me," I said to Tokie, readying my inactgun.

"*You* stay close to Birken," a voice grunted, and I turned to see Tokie had turned back into the Trecian male.

I could take care of myself, but she did have a point. My looks weren't as intimidating as hers . . . I mean, his. Taking a breath, I stepped forward and let the distant hunger choose our path.

We turned down narrow streets, and at times, when the buildings were too tall and shadowed the little light we had, I had to depend on Tokie/Birken's eyesight. Thieves, rapists and other ruffians approached and challenged us. Fortunately, the armaments on Quuto were almost exactly like that of my home world. Not many automatic weapons were available. Beings fought mostly with clubs and knives, but the Ja'pah's field sprouted up to protect us from those who did have ejecting weaponry. Plus, with my gun and fighting skills and Birken's strength, we were able to keep them at bay. I couldn't imagine having to live on this planet all my life, fighting every day and hour. No wonder every Being that we saw was like an animal--fight or flight.

Suddenly, as we turned another corner of twisted mazes, I stopped still, feeling . . . something.

"What is this?" I heard a voice behind us, cold and inimical.

I was too frozen to turn to look at the intimidator, but Birken faced the new hostile. "What are you?"

"We ask the questions," the voice ordered. "You invade on our property, you must pay us toll."

Snapping away the unnamed feeling that wanted me to go forward, I forced myself to turn around and face fifteen males blocking the way that we had come. Behind us was a dead end, a metal wall sprayed with graffiti. Because my feet were not cooperating, I had only my voice. But when I opened my mouth and tried to speak, no sound came out.

"How much we pay?" Birken croaked.

"All that you have, and then more after that." The leader pawed his knife. "We'll take the female for a bonus."

Birken pulled me behind him. "Female mine."

"She's financial liability," he said with a nod, and his comrades began to approach.

Realizing I was frozen with fear, Birken grabbed my inactgun and lurched forward. He was able to hold off five males, but his strength was waning too quickly. I was only able to move one step back as I watched them pile on him, swinging downward blows. The rest walked towards me with baleful smiles.

I awoke from my stupor too late. They trammeled me to the ground and six of them urged the one in front to proceed with the fun. With a heckling laugh, he bent forward and tugged at my pants.

A bolt of light sprayed through the air, and the one stooped over me flew backward and collided into a side wall. Shouts rang out as the males scampered about to find who was firing at them. I jumped up, jabbing at a few who were still near and looked around for Tokie. Bodies spurted by me in chaotic lines, and my eyes fixed themselves upon three stationary Beings at the dead end of the alley, their cloaks waving in the air.

The flitting shadows were soon out of the alley, and I was alone with the three rescuers. Tokie was nowhere to be seen.

"You seem to get yourself in the most detrimental situations," the familiar Voice spoke and the three-cloaked saviors walked in unison towards me.

I wanted to gape at the red, blue and green colors, but my caustic side won over. "Voice. Surprised to see you again."

"Mutual." He nodded, his two brothers stopping just behind him. "Another coincidence?"

I held my tongue. No, it wasn't. This was too synchronal to be a coincidence.

"Well, it doesn't matter," Voice opened his arms. "You have two choices: one, do as we ask, or two, do as we state."

Espy moved, coming closer and ahead of Voice. "Please, will you come with me?"

I stepped back and tried to stall. "Perhaps we should talk about this?" Steic! Where was Tokie?

Voice lifted his hooded head. "I'm afraid not."

I felt a pinch on my thigh, and I looked down and saw a blue splotch. Reso was near me, holding a weapon in his hand, and suddenly the alley began to whirl.

The last words that I heard came from Voice. "You should have taken the first choice, Jetticia."

# # #

I awoke to see black spikes zooming towards me. Immediately, I jumped out of the way, falling awkwardly to the floor.

"Didn't mean to frighten you," a voice said as I looked up to see the Hyperian physician. "Please. Sit back down." He patted the white chair. "I haven't finished your examination."

I was back in the white room with no walls or exits. The Hyperian sat on his lifted stool. The fact that I was still alive was promising.

"Voice. Is he here?" I stood up, certain that he was somewhere, watching.

"Please. Your examination."

I had forgotten, the Hyperian's mouth was shut like clasped metal, molten together. Perhaps I should try another tactic. "What are you examining? I feel fine."

He waved towards the chair.

I gave in and sat back down. "If you start with that massaging thing, I'll rip one of your spikes off."

"At this time of season, I think that would be quite hard to do." He waved his hands around his spikes.

I did notice that they were a lot larger than normal. "Found anyone who would take you on?"

"Many," he bragged. "The females were practically fighting to have my seeds. I am of top quality. My spikes are harder and longer than the best of them, and my mind is a strong mental structure."

"How many?" I stroked his ego.

"Fifteen. My seeds are growing as we speak."

"Suphyz has touched and blessed you well."

"Indeed. And She you."

I didn't know how to take that, being that I was a hostage of the Ja'pah's Minions, and being a half-breed wasn't a blessing at all. I didn't reply to that compliment, so I remained silent instead. Sitting back in the chair, I allowed him to wave his hands over me, but he did not touch me.

The Minions returned once my "examination" was over. The Hyperian left immediately, leaving us alone.

"I trust you are feeling well." Voice pulled back his hood, his pleasing features bringing color to the white room.

"I wasn't ill," I answered, sitting up and getting out of the chair. "Shall we get on with it?"

"With . . . it?" Voice was sly with his words.

I had to be careful to say little and not display too much. "With whatever you plan to do with me."

"Ahhh, yes." He beckoned Espy forward.

I stood still. Would they decide to kill me now? Allow me to become comfortable with my life and then take it away from me?

"Please go with my brother. He will tend to you." Voice turned to leave.

"Tend to me how, might I ask?"

He didn't answer as Reso followed him to the exit. They disappeared through a door of some sort that blended in with the white room. I looked at Espy and glanced back at the portal.

His hood slightly lifted. "I see your discomfort. You mustn't be."

I knew he could see the blood cells coursing through my veins, and my heart pumping adrenaline throughout my body. "If you were in my place, how would you feel?"

He beckoned towards the exit. "I would fear."

I swallowed, knowing that I had to keep thinking if I was going to get out of this situation. But with Minions as my escorts, what could I do? I slipped out of the chair and walked towards the portal.

# # #

Immediately, I was at the entryway of a ship, and I knew then that we had just left a planet. Portals like these were rare and expensive. Steic, everything that the Minions did was expensive! I could only guess that I was on Hyperone, the Hyperian's home world, which was also located in the Second Quadrant, and which had the most advanced medical technology of all Four Quadrants.

Espy walked up beside me and edged me forward. He took me to the pilot room and sat down. From the entryway and the distance we traveled throughout the hallways to the pilot room, I assumed the ship's occupancy was for three or four Beings. Pushing a few controls, Espy had the ship soon on its way.

The stars blinked as we slipped into inner space. This ship was unique, indeed--it could fly fast and slip through space without even an hour of preparation. Then again, it was probably left in operation, waiting for its pilots' return. Darkness surrounded us for some moments before the stars reappeared again. We had flown with a speed at which I had never known and slipped through space in what felt like no time at all. The stars were like any other stars, yet we could be anywhere.

We blinked again, and then again, and soon became surrounded in a field of meteoroids. I gasped, knowing it was dangerous to be here, yet Espy flew the ship deftly. As I found myself beginning to trust his skill, I then tensed again when I saw a meteoroid heading directly in our path. I barely had time to flinch as Espy didn't avoid it. We slammed right into the rock, and a blinding flash lit up the ship. Then everything was still.

I finally remembered to breathe again, looking out the window and seeing that we were now surrounded by walls. We had landed!

Espy escorted me outside, and I stared in amazement at the small terminal with white walls and strange lights glittering on the floor. From the size of the station, I guessed it could hold four more crafts the same size as Espy's.

"We're inside the meteoroid?"

Espy never answered, but I knew I was right. Steic, the entire rock field could have been an illusion. This was their crypt; I knew it. It had to be. *How many have lain eyes on their sequestered hideout?* I wondered. *What secrets did this place hold?*

"Is this your crypt, Espy? You and your brothers'? The Ja'pah?" I asked, though I knew he wouldn't admit to it.

"This way," he indicated instead of answering, and I followed him out of the terminal down a grand hallway.

We arrived at the end of the hallway, which branched off into three dark directions. He led me to the right, passing through a room with a large black marble table aligned with four matching high-backed chairs. He then escorted me around the corner and down another hall with a large door that opened as we approached. Espy stepped to the side and allowed me to enter first.

I should have been wary, but I went ahead, too enthralled by my surroundings to heed my instinctual caution. As soon as I passed the threshold, the door slammed shut behind me. Trapped. I turned around, suddenly realizing that Espy was not at my side. I palmed the panel, which should have opened the door, but it remained locked.

"Fantastic. Espy, if you're out there," I shouted, hoping the door wasn't soundproof, "I hope you're having a good laugh." I waved at the door, knowing he could probably see right through it. Finally giving up, I turned around and my eyes widened.

A large four-poster bed stood in the middle of the room, stacked with pillows and draped with glittering silk. To the side was a small pool that gurgled with different-colored lights, turning the water into a mesmerizing kaleidoscope of colors. A large dressing area was to the left, next to a small eating table with two plush chairs, and a massive white vase decorated one corner. Closer to me was a lounge area with a long curved sitting sofa, facing a glass table which was probably a univice and holoscreen combined in one.

"Very rich, Espy," I shouted towards the door, "but it's still a prison!"

I went straight to the glass table and sat down on the comfortable sofa. "Bymé, position?"

"Sorry, Jetta," Bymé answered. "I'm unable to comply. There have been restrictions placed upon my operation."

Of course. "So what's your limit? What can you show me on this thing?"

"It seems I'm limited to entertainment sources only."

"No news?"

"Yes, I am able to comply with that order. One moment."

"No, Bymé, Ti'senot. I'm not in the mood for entertainment."

I paced the room, trying to figure out why I kept running into Minions. If Tokie were here, she would most likely come up with some ridiculous idea. In her inimitable way, she would probably even hint that one of them was . . . which was utterly ridiculous. I turned and stared at the closed door. Was it ridiculous? Could one of them be . . . no, of course not! There had to be another explanation.

I looked down at the Qutcy and decided that *it* was the problem. The brothers had signaled me to come, but why? And why bring me here? Were they interested in playing games with lives? Looking around the room, it seemed to be made for me, or at least for a female. They were male, after all. Perhaps the hunger was some sort of trick to make me think I was in Calling so that they, or at least one of them, could enjoy limitless, free sexual pleasure. If they even *thought* I was going to prostitute myself, I would make sure they would rethink their plans.

Hours passed with no contact from Espy. I lay down, tired of pacing and snooping around the room. There wasn't anything to see anyway. There were clothes, a replicator for food, that huge vase to decorate the corner of the room--all there, it seemed, for my peace and ease. It was a comfortable cell with all the high tech to go along with it, which told me that my stay was going to be a long one.

"Perhaps some xaronae?" Bymé suddenly suggested.

"Some what?"

An arrow on my Qutcy pointed to the small table. Sitting on top of it was a black-and-red striped box. Oddly, I hadn't noticed it before. I went towards it, picked it up and opened it. Inside were six rolls of black, round objects.

"How do you eat it?" I asked Bymé, picking one up and examining its soft shell.

"It contents are entirely edible. It is a delicacy treasured by most Beings in all Four Quadrants."

Sniffing the large black objects, I could smell the sweetness and bit into it. Inside, white cream coating and a red, thick jelly began to slowly drip down on my fingertips. I plopped the rest of it into my mouth, feeling the shell melt away, and the jelly filled my mouth with its sweet, fruity taste. I ate all six rolls, feeling my insides tingle joyously.

# # #

Hours turned into days, and the only company I had was Bymé and the holoscreen, which at least kept me in touch with the outside world. My mind began to decelerate from lack of stimulus, causing me to hear things, like the door opening, and I would jump out to see who it was, but the room never changed. Several times I tried to have Bymé contact someone from outside, but she insisted that no one was there and that she couldn't communicate with anyone outside the meteoroid.

So, I was left on a rock, incarcerated in a luxurious room. I realized it could be worse, but it was slowly turning wretched. For the first time, I felt alone. I always had somewhere to go, someone to see, and I always had the option to go home. I was never alone, and I had never been lonely.

As the days turned into weeks, I had almost forgotten about my hunger pains, which seemed to have completely disappeared. This made me believe that the Minions had probably prodded it out of me in the first place. Though the pains were no longer an issue, I didn't think I could handle the solitude much longer. If this was their tactic of provoking me to comply with being a pleasure servant, it was surely working. Depression was setting in, slowly eroding my spirit.

I began wearing the same soft robe every day and bathing only when it was absolutely necessary. It didn't matter how I looked or smelled anyway, as there was no one around. My only comfort was the sweet delicacy, xaronae, which Bymé had ready for me to eat every morning. It was the only thing I looked forward to.

I began to sleep through most of what would have been the day, and Bymé would then repeatedly tell me that it was time to wake up. I finally ordered her to leave me alone, and I began to sleep most of the night as well, until my body became restless and tired, leaving me to pace the room the rest of the night.

Sometimes I idly browsed through the news, but the notion of the world outside, and me inside, was becoming unbearable.

Next, frustration set in, and I began tearing up the room. I threw anything that was movable on the floor, and anything light enough to fly through the air. And then there was that enormous vase. I pounded myself into it until the pain in my shoulder became unbearable. But it never budged. I destroyed everything tangible, only to have it put back in place the next morning when awoke. When I inquired, Bymé said she was able to do it with the aid of some devices she had found, but she wouldn't tell me where or what they were. So, tearing up the room became a routine that I indulged in every other day. There was nothing else to do.

Finally a day came when I managed to break the vase, and the crash it caused when it tumbled over and scattered into several pieces, shocked me. Somehow, after gorging on xaronae, I had built such anger, such strength, that my pounding finally sent it falling to the floor.

After several moments of silence, Bymé announced, "You have been invited to attend dinner with your hosts. Please be ready within the hour."

Chapter 9   Minions

I thought about going to dinner in my robe and unwashed body, but then decided not to show that the solitude had affected me in any way. After bathing in the pool and draping myself again with the soft robe, I prepared my hair and chose a white dress for the occasion. When I was ready, I sat on the edge of the bed, waiting for one of the Minions to retrieve me.

No one arrived. Another game, perhaps?

I wanted to tear up the room again, and then suddenly the door opened. Cautiously, I walked towards it, expecting it to close as soon as I came too near, but it remained open, and I quickly ran through it, feeling like a slave running toward freedom. There was only one direction, which, if I had remembered correctly, led to the large dining room.

They were all there, the three Minions, sitting at the table, upon which was enough food for a small feast.

"Ahhh, Jetticia, there you are," Voice greeted me as if he had just spoken to me the day before. "Please, join us."

I took the one empty seat at the end of the table opposite Voice, who sat at the other end. He was the only one who did not wear his hood. Espy, in his green cowl, sat to my left, and Reso, in blue, to my right. Without another word, they began to eat, and from the way their bodies moved from time to time, I could tell they were mentally speaking with each other. I ate slowly and deliberately, my senses secretly delighting on the live company. I didn't need them to speak to me; I was simply content just to have someone there, and they probably knew that.

When they finished their meal, I continued to nibble on mine, trying to extend my stay as long as I could. I looked for more to eat and saw a bowl of xaronae just out of my reach. I yearned for them.

Looking next to my plate, I noticed a device that brought food near my area and pressed the button, which was decorated with a symbol similar to the one on the bowl. The xaronae came slowly in my direction, and my insides convulsed. Voice glanced up at me but then returned to his discussion with his brothers, and for a moment I hesitated to take one of the xaronae. As I eyed the black shells, my craving overwhelmed my suspicions, and I ate every round bit of sweetness in the bowl.

Then, pain seared through me.

It hit me with no forewarning, not even an inkling, and I fell right out of my chair with a muffled scream. The Minions jumped up and ran to me, and I grabbed the first gloved hand I saw.

"Please, help me."

Espy was frozen as I clung to his hand.

"Espy!" Voice shouted for his attention.

Slowly, the green hood looked up toward Voice.

Voice grabbed Espy's wrist and tugged his hand away from mine. "Help us carry her to her room. Don't look at her."

They lifted me up physically and mentally so that my weight was not completely on their arms. Struggling, I tried to fight my hunger, but the moans escaped my hold. They settled me down on my bed, and one of them stuck something in my arm. With strength I didn't know I had, I shoved one of them away. The blue cloak fell down, his legs wildly sprawling about.

"Reso!" Voice exclaimed.

I fell into darkness.

# # #

When I awoke, the room was silent. The room was always silent, but it seemed even more quiet than usual. I sat up, noticing that what I had worn the previous night had been replaced with a pink nightgown. My skin felt soft and smooth, and my insides seemed to hum in comfort. Raking my hands through my hair, I sat up, bewildered, trying to figure out what was wrong . . . no, different.

I looked around the room trying to see what had changed, but everything remained as it always had. Yet something felt different. No, no, *I* felt different. I touched my arms and my thighs, and my forearm brushed against my breasts. It was then that I knew. I should have known it when I first woke up.

Someone had lain with me.

I smelled my arms, and then the sheets, and then the pillows, but everything smelled clean and fresh.

"Those vulgar, sessling . . . Bymé!"

"Yes, Jetta?" Bymé cordially answered.

"Who was in my bed last night?"

"You have been asleep for the past three nights. Please specify which one."

"Three nights? Three nights! Who did it, Bymé? Which one was in my bed!"

"I'm sorry, Jetta, I don't fully understand--"

"You know what I'm talking about, Bymé. Who was it? Who slept with me? Bymé! Fleik! Steic!" I threw the pillows off the bed, got up, and turned over the tables and chairs. "Who was it, Bymé? Espy? Reso? Voice? Or did they all take turns?"

Bymé didn't answer me as I broke everything in the room that was breakable, and when I tripped over my own feet and fell on the floor, she replied, "I don't have any recordings of the events about which you are inquiring."

Of course she didn't, which made me furious. Never any answers! Only questions! My eyes searched for something else to release my anger, but I had already broken everything I could, so I broke them again, until small, shattered pieces surrounded me. Growling and screaming, I made as much of a mess as possible until I fell to the floor, exhausted. Then, the door opened and Reso stepped in.

I hissed at him, too tired to even attempt to lunge an attack. "Looking in on your conquered game?"

His hood gazed over the entire room and then rested on me.

"So, how was I? Did you enjoying hearing me moan, or did I just breathe very heavily? I'm sure you got an earful."

"We're not savages, Jetticia," he finally spoke, his voice calm and almost soothing.

"Really? So, which turn were you, Minion? Or do you just like to listen?"

He didn't answer, but turned to go.

I stormed after him, wanting to tear his blue cloak to shreds. Reso stepped aside so smoothly, it was almost soundless. I lost my balance and fell out into the hallway.

"You're too noisy," he said, stepping over me, and continued walking down the hall. "We'll need to work on that."

I imagined zapping him with my inactgun and using a metal object with very sharp edges to trim his hood. The anger slowly amplified inside me, increasing like an expanding bubble, and suddenly it released with a pop.

The Minion stumbled.

Whipping his hood around, he looked back at me.

I sneered at him, ravishing in the Minion's bluster. He quickly turned the corner. I wish I could take credit for his clumsiness, but there wasn't any way I could touch a Minion. Yet somehow, I would make them pay for what they did.

"This isn't over, Minion!" I shouted at him, knowing he heard me before scattering off in the direction that led to the terminal.

I sat in the grand hallway for some time, trying to regain strength to collide with the entire meteoroid. But when I got up and moved into the dining area, I suddenly realized I was alone again. Going to the landing area proved it. It was empty. Yet, I did notice one thing . . ..

I was free.

I paused for a moment, considering that feeling, and then I questioned the reasoning behind it. Perhaps Reso felt guilty about . . . Bymé said three nights? Three nights. One of them, or all of them, had me, and then decided to reward me? The thought sent more venom through my veins, and I put that idea aside. Either way, I finally had free reign of the place, and if I found anything personal, I was destroying it.

As I traced my steps back down the grand hallway, I turned left instead of right, away from the dining room and my cell. When I entered a large room with three doors, I immediately realized where I was--by their private chambers. The doors were red, green and blue. The three colors merged to a point at the middle of the ceiling and flowed down to the base of the floor, precisely aligned.

I walked to the red door and placed my hand on the panel, though I knew it would be locked. I tried the other two door panels anyway. Having no luck, I decided to go back to the grand hallway and this time went straight ahead, toward the other end of the terminal. Darkness surrounded me until I went through an archway and heard the almost happy, gurgling sounds of water. A marble white and black fountain sat in the middle of a room, molded into twisting masses of smooth rods spiraling up several feet in the air. It stood in front of stairways that led up to black double doors lined with huge pillars.

I slowly realized . . . those were *his* doors. The Ja'pah.

Large, heinous beasts with bared teeth and muscled bodies on four legs clung to two posts aligning the stairs. I circled the fountain to get a closer look, and suddenly their eyes began to glow, and I heard snarling. The creatures leapt from their posts, their teeth dripping and clenching; claws ready to rend. With stealth, they approached me.

I backed away very slowly, thinking that if I didn't make any sudden movements, they wouldn't pounce. They followed me with threatening gestures until I passed the archway, and then they stood their ground, waiting for me to walk back down the hallway, which I did willingly.

I was gasping when I flew into my room, and for the first time, I was grateful for the closed door. Though the beasts hadn't followed me past the archway, their presence was so strong that I felt as if they had. I locked the door and stood, nearly frozen. That's probably what those steic Minions thought I would do anyway. Those beasts obviously ran wild through the meteoroid, and I was still a prisoner.

In time, the solitude dissipated my fear and anger, and I began to wonder about my predicament. Locking me in a room was one thing, but I was a thief, and giving me free reign meant I had possibilities. Then, I remembered there were no ships. Nonetheless, there had to be options.

As I thought of the items available to me, my mind kept going back to the Minions' behavior and the words they had said to me. Espy said they weren't savages. What did that mean? Did they think just because all three were united by the Ja'pah's blood that they were actually only one Being, and that lying with me was normal? Or did only one lay with me?

My actions that had brought me here, my intense hunger, all of it, Tokie believed, had to do with The Calling. And Tokie was right about how it had affected my mother. Was this Suphyz's way of letting me know? Was I indeed in Calling? Was one of the Minions my True Mate?

I had to admit, it made sense. My hunger had led me to them. I had searched them out every single time. What else could they do but lock me up in a rock and keep me there? I was a risk to their operations. The Ja'pah was Wendh himself, and I was sure he would not kill a fellow Wendh who had a Calling for one of his Minions.

By the Name!

There wouldn't be any other reason to keep me here. To keep me alive. To lie with me.

One of them *was* my True Mate. But which one? They were all together on each of the planets, and also at the dinner. It was obvious they didn't want me to know which one. When the hunger gnawed at me, they made sure they were all present.

I started pondering the possibilities.

Perhaps it was Espy. He was always the one I was alone with, and Voice did command him not to look at me, after all. He was taken in by my pain when I was in hunger. He wanted me; I saw it.

But then again, it could be Voice. He was handsome and equal to my stubbornness. He was the leader of the three, and I did like his polite aggressiveness. Yet he could be shielding Reso.

Reso was the Minion with whom I had the least contact. I knew nothing about him and had barely heard him speak. But then again, he barely spoke anyway.

Pondering over who could be my True Mate agitated me. They must know I would find out eventually. The Calling would point me to the right one; there was no stopping that.

But still, I was confused: Why didn't they want me to know?

# # #

Days later, I awoke, but not in my cell. Espy stood over me, his green cloak casting a shadow. I sat up, noticing that I was again in a white room, but this time I was lying on the floor.

"I need you to get that flower for me," Espy calmly said.

I didn't know what the steic he was talking about. "You treat me like a bawd and now you want me to fetch for you?" Though I knew their secret now, I wasn't going to let on that I had figured it out. "Ti'senot, Espy. Get it yourself."

I soon regretted my pompous attitude as a flaring fire shot through my veins, descending from a purple light in the ceiling.

"The flower," Espy repeated.

I gritted my teeth as I allowed the stinging pain to subside. This wasn't the proper way to treat one's mate, and I almost blurted that out.

I breathed slowly.

Espy allowed me to get my bearings before I stood, cursed and looked around the room for the fleiking flower. The flower was at the opposite end of the room. Its purple petals almost glowed in the brilliant white room. Looking at Espy, I cursed under my breath again and marched straight toward the flower. While still muttering curses, something sprung up from the floor, making me jump to the side, ready for attack. It was a blunt blade that immediately retracted back into the floor. I snapped around and glared at Espy, who stood calmly where I had left him.

This was a test. Like the fleiking Reuss. I should have known. If it weren't for that purple light, I wouldn't play along with this stupid game.

With more caution, I took another step, trying to locate the triggers for the blades, but nothing was immediately noticeable. After I took another step, something sprung from the wall, which I dodged by rolling away, only to jump back to my feet when another blade shot up from the floor.

I wasn't fast enough. The blade stung as it hit the side of my leg. With more determination, I ran towards the flower, leaping and twisting to avoid the objects that flew from the ceiling, the walls and the floors.

I was hit a few times before I was able to grab the flower from the wall, but the obstacle course wasn't over.

The room came alive with bars, tunnels and nets. Something swung in the distance, and I smelled something burning.

"This is ridiculous." I felt like I was back at The Mill.

Stuffing the flower in my shirt, I jumped up to the first bar, barely missing a foul-smelling, sticky glob that shot through the air. I swung around, jumped on another rod and tilted a little to gain my balance. I walked across it, arms slightly out for stability, only to fall off when something sprung up from the floor and hit me on the shoulder.

I landed feet first and started running. Speed made me think faster, without second guessing myself. I could leap and turn and roll almost by instinct, and before I knew it, I had made it across and stood in front of Espy again, bruised, clothing partly burned and torn, blood trickling from my flesh and out of breath.

I dropped the flower into his outstretched hand, and he held it up to the darkness in the hood, inhaling its fragrance.

"Poor eyesight. You'll have to do better." He turned and walked through a now open door that led to the landing area.

I was still inside the meteoroid, somewhere on the other side, though at first I thought perhaps I was back on the Hyperian's ship. Turning around, I looked at the room, which was again white and empty. I didn't hear the devices return to their places. And I didn't hear Espy leave in his ship.

# # #

Reso woke me two nights later in the same white room.

"I haven't recovered from the first test," I complained. "What is this about, anyway? You want me to do a cate for you or something?"

Reso remain quiet as usual, his blue cloak shimmering. He pulled back his hood and dropped his cowl to the ground, and there, suddenly exposed, were the most enormous ears I had ever seen on a living creature. They were slightly blue in color, downed with short hair fuzz. Both ears curved upward from the top of his head and flowed down his back to dangle near his feet. With ears like that, no wonder he could hear so keenly.

I stood stunned, looking at a face that no one had ever seen before. Black, small, beady eyes blinked at me, and his head was speckled with spots of thick black hair like a Quattor, but he had two arms instead of four. He wore a body suit that matched his blue cloak and blended with his pale blue skin. I also couldn't help noticing that it also highlighted the muscled curves of his body. He was so fit and so well defined, I found myself swallowing so as not to drool.

"Follow my directions exactly." Reso spoke softly and then began to move his pale, strong arms in a wave-like motion and shifted his feet slightly, his muscled legs tensing and releasing. He looked as if he were dancing in water as he turned and swayed, balancing on one foot and then on his toes.

Stopping suddenly before me, he snapped his fingers in my face, jerking me out of my stupor. "Follow me," he whispered.

Hesitant, I did as I was instructed, knowing that he would probably use the purple ray of fire on me if I didn't. The dance was complicated and strenuous, though it had looked simple. Reso reproved me from time to time: I was too "noisy," and squealing babes could hear me over their own crying. I tried to be as silent as possible, but it never was good enough.

When he finally said, "Now we may rest," I fell to the ground exhausted, no longer interested and too tired to gawk at his body. I didn't get up until a few hours later, when I realized I had drifted off to sleep.

# # #

I continued with my odd training for months, with Reso and Espy alternating their lessons. Each kept his distance from me, but I was overwhelmed by the beauty of both of them.

I liked Reso gentleness, and his body was a sculpture. Yet Espy's skill in fighting was an art in itself, but I had never seen under his hood. The only contact I had with Voice was over the unicomm, as he was mostly out on excursions.

Voice's instructed me to read certain history lessons and keep up on current news for several planets at the same time. He would then quiz me when I wasn't prepared, which sometimes resulted in a purple light of punishment. Reso was the only Minion of the thre who didn't use pain as discipline, but that didn't mean he was the one to whom I was being Called. Voice would sometimes withhold xaronae from me for a few days when he felt I was being unruly, which drove me nearly insane with hunger.

I would stuff myself for an hour when I finally did receive the sweet delicacy, disgusted with myself for my addiction, but the xaronae made me feel like myself again.

I was becoming the xaronae's slave, and their slave, through this sweet delight, and though I knew this, I couldn't stop myself and never tried to fight it. It kept me calm and at peace, and it pacified my hunger, thus keeping The Calling away for long periods of time. When it wouldn't ease my hunger and my desire broke through, all three Minions would arrive and invite me to dinner, place the xaronae in front of me to eat, and I would wake the next day, my body refreshed, feeling deliciously energized, with no memory of who had quenched my hunger.

Chapter 10   Negotiations

"Put this on." Espy threw something soft on my lap.

I finished yet another box of xaronae, stood up from the sofa and lifted the white cloth in my hands. It was heavy and shimmering. Turning it around, I found a hood and sleeves and immediately recognized it as a cowl.

"Why?" I stared at Espy.

"Wear this underneath it." He threw another soft object at me and then pointed to the floor. "Put those on," he pointed, and I saw some boot-like footwear.

"Meet me at the landing bay," he instructed, leaving me bewildered.

The one-piece undergarment hugged my body quite comfortably, flowing down to my elbows and knees. The white cloak engulfed all of me except for my hands, and though the hood was completely dark inside, I could see everything around me clearly. After dressing, I told Bymé to display a hologram of myself.

I yanked the hood from my head. "By the Name! I look like a Minion."

"Yes. You do," Bymé replied. "Espy is ordering that you hurry."

Was this what the training was all about? Did they want to recruit a sister Minion? But why? Why me?

I ran out of the room and headed for the landing bay, hoping that wherever we were going would give me some answers. There was only one ship, its door wide open, and I went inside.

"Be more prompt next time," Espy commanded while hitting the controls to take flight "And put those on."

Sitting on the chair next to him were two white gloves. I picked them up. "What's going on? Where are you taking me?"

"Silence, Jetta." He never turned away from the controls. "You are to remain silent and keep your eyes open."

I sat down next to him, feeling slightly excited as I do with most cates, yet my mind buzzed with questions.

We flew out of the meteoroid cluster and the stars winked as we zapped into inner space, arriving at a space station in what seemed like no time at all. It was as large as a planet, lights flickering around it and on its massive hull. It appeared as if buildings upon buildings were mashed together, high-rises shelving uncountable levels and multiple bridges with uneven rooftops.

"Deluxar," I whisper aloud, awed at its sight and beauty. I had seen its shape on holoscreens, but I had never dreamed I would see it with my own eyes. It floated on the edge of the Fourth Quadrant, almost hidden from planetary life forms.

"There was a planet here once," Espy said quietly, "but it was destroyed in the Xarthren War. It's quite similar to your residing planet Hentpki--a mixture of several species all in one place."

"What are we doing here?" I tried to squeeze in a question, taking the opportunity of Espy's willingness to converse, but the question only reminded him of his duty.

"Put on your hood and never take it off. In fact, you should keep it on as soon as we leave our home site." Espy guided his ship into Deluxar without another word.

We didn't gain entrance to Deluxar with proper clearance, nor did we land in a terminal. A small tunnel projected out from a secluded side of the space station, and Espy's ship was small enough to pass through. Someone on the inside gave him entrance, and we were suddenly part of a sky full of ships and two-seater galers flying around in the interior of Deluxar. It was night here, and I wondered if the day and night intervals were like on Quuto.

We flew for almost an hour before landing inside the crack of a building that sealed immediately upon our entry.

"Silence," Espy reminded me, and I suddenly began to feel uneasy.

I walked behind him out of the ship and saw that we had company. A Being stood in the dark terminal, waiting to escort us to our destination, and I immediately saw this assembly for what it was. A meeting. A very important and deadly meeting. Sadotch and Vrang held these types of meetings all of the time, though I was never a part of them, and never wanted to be. They were too intense, too risky, and could too easily erupt into violence.

And I felt the intensity in the air.

Why the fleik was I here?

We followed our escort, who was of a species I didn't recognize. His bald head told me nothing, but the hair protruding from the rim of his shirt told me that he could be a descendant of some half-dozen of hairy species. He didn't speak as we went through twisted hallways and entered a room where two more Beings sat waiting. It was too dark to see what, or who, they were, but I supposed that was best.

Espy and I took our places at the two remaining empty seats, which were more like stools, with four legs and no backs. It was safer that way. No hidden gadgets to spring up and restrain us.

One of the Beings leaned forward. "So this is your new company."

"The codes," Espy announced.

"I have them," the male voice answered. "Do you have what I need?"

"Here."

"And I have the crystals," a female voice entered the conversation.

I cringed at the sound of the word "crystals." She could only be talking about reoet crystals. This was not good.

Espy and the other attendees placed their items upon a round table in front of the four of us: a black box and two translucent casings for cubes containing a large amount of information. The table turned and the items stopped in front of each recipient.

Something wasn't right; I looked up, sensing something.

Espy reached forward, and I yanked his arm back. Something blasted out of the ceiling, hitting the space where Espy's hand had been. Everyone jumped up and searched for the attacker. Espy sailed through the air, his arms straight up. He broke through the ceiling and scraps of metal fell down as he clasped a head and brought it down hard. The assassin's body fell from the ceiling, landing flat on the floor, and Espy held him still with his mind as he floated in the air. It was important that the assassin didn't move, not even an inch, or he'd end his own life before we could get any answers. I immediately recognized him as the hairy male who had met us in the small terminal.

I turned to the other two in the room and saw the woman staring at the other attendee with shocked anger, but the male took a slight step backward. Instinct took over as I crossed the room in one step and wrapped my arm around his neck, holding him secure.

"What are you doing?" the male shouted. "Espy, call your brethren away! Doesn't he know who I am?"

Espy looked up from the assassin and floated down to the floor. "I believe my sister thinks you're behind this."

"I am not. I had nothing to do--"

I squeezed harder on his throat.

"Stop! It wasn't me!"

The female came closer and sniffed him. "I smell a traitor and a liar. Fader!"

"No!" He fervently protested. "I-I was here too. He tried to kill me as well."

"Silence!" The female commanded and went for his eyes.

I pulled him away from her vengeful hands and looked towards Espy. His head tilted slightly and the assassin on the floor split in half. I turned my eyes away.

"I want his eyes, Minion!" The female threatened me, moving closer to the fader. I could see her yellow eyes burning in vengeance.

"I believe my master would like a word with him first," I answered. By the Name! She called me Minion?

Espy crossed over to us and stood next to the female. "We will take him. You can keep the crystals in exchange for this, and I will also give you his codes."

"I have no use for codes," the female said, turning away. "We will need to meet again for some . . . other items. But I will keep the crystals."

She grabbed the black box off the table and left the room hastily. I wanted to follow her example just in case there was another assassin in the area. Espy tilted his head slightly again, and the male in my arms went limp. Mentally, he took the male from my arms and floated him in the air.

"The codes," he ordered, and I went to the table to retrieve them. We walked swiftly back to the ship and escaped from Deluxar.

Espy placed the fader in a black oval tube, and sealed it shut before returning to the ship's panels. I couldn't sit; my nerves were still actively pulsing in my body. "Espy?" I said with a slight plea in my voice.

I didn't think he would answer, but surprisingly he asked, "How did you know?"

"I--" I began before actually thinking of the answer, but I heard myself saying, "I sensed something there, above us."

Espy nodded, but I didn't understand it at all. "You did well." His compliment warmed my insides and calmed my agitation, but it returned with his next comment. "Next time, do not take action, and do not speak when I tell you to be silent."

Objection rose fiercely in my voice. "You were too busy with the assassin! What did you have me there for anyway? I couldn't sit there and watch! You would be sizzling right now if it weren't for me!"

Espy turned around. "It wasn't supposed to happen that way."

"Well, Espy, it did! With this kind of business, anything could happen, everything is risky! You've been doing this forever! You should know that!"

He turned back around and said, "I cannot have you damaged in any way. You must value your life more than mine. You must be more careful, Jetticia."

"Fleik! What is that supposed to mean?" I threw the cubes in the chair. "I didn't make a mistake back there! I believe it was you!"

Espy sealed his lips, and I stormed to the back of the ship to get as far away from him as possible.

I didn't need to be escorted back to my room when we had reached the meteoroid; I was first out of the ship. Throwing off the cloak, I kicked the bedpost and fell unhindered on the bed. I hoped Espy wasn't my True Mate; he drove me insane with anger. Reso, on the other hand, had a calming effect over me. Perhaps he was my True Mate. Yet my reactions towards Espy was probably typical for mates. Espy did seem to have a sincere concern for me, but he may have just wanted me to protect myself for his brother, whichever one that may be.

Shaking my head, I decided to stop pondering on True Mate issues and dwell on my first cate for the Ja'pah, which was a complete disaster. My first day as . . . as sister Minion? The thought made me smile.

Then I realized--that was how they were going to explain me to the public. It was quite ingenious, actually. The best way to hold a secret was to keep it open, for all to see. Also, it looked like they needed more help anyway, and now that I thought about it, being a Minion wouldn't be so bad. Celebrity had its appeal, and the wealth was overwhelming. I would be known as part of the Ja'pah, though I hadn't finished all of my training and doubted if I would ever taste the Ja'pah's blood to actually become his Minion.

As I dozed off, I wondered hazily if, once I had actually joined with my mate, whether the Ja'pah's blood would affect me as well. And what role would I play in this small, elite club?

# # #

I woke up with a slight panic, hearing whisperings above me. My eyes flew open, expecting to see all three Minions hovering over me, discussing the punishment for my disobedience, but no one was in my room. Yet the whisperings continued.

". . . and she's becoming too strong. We can't hold her much longer." It was Espy's voice, and it was coming from inside my head!

"We need more time," Voice was anxious. "It has taken us too long to find out why The Lady was kidnapped. The codes must be true if Wryne tried to have you killed so that you would not possess them."

"Wryne was weak," Reso's voice was soft even in my mind. "But whoever put him up to it was clever. They told the Isdollem nothing so that he had nothing to tell us. Whoever found out about the meeting must have known that we are trying to intervene."

"They knew someone was intervening when The Lady was rescued from that kidnapping at the Hotel Quitimah," Voice snapped. "We must act quickly. Vortsi must receive these codes to gain entry into Isdol. We have wasted too much time already."

"Brother," Reso soothed, "I know you abide by Wendh traditions, but I insist that Maheir Vortsi should not go to Isdol--"

"You have already expressed your view, Reso. We will revive Vortsi and allow him to continue on his mission, and we---"

Reso interrupted, "And we should go in his place instead."

There was silence, and then Espy encouraged, "Go on."

"It is too risky to have Vortsi on Isdol," Reso explained. "His death will only cause more delays."

Suddenly, I felt a surge of power so overwhelming, I grabbed the edge of the bed, but at the same time, I was drawn to it. It covered me with a slight smothering sensation, and my urge, my hunger, leapt up. I found myself inadvertently walking out of my room, rounding the corner and staring at the three Minions sitting at the table.

All three had thrown back their hoods, and I saw Espy for the first time. His eyes were enormous. They were about the same size as his ears, and they were the most beautiful emeralds I have ever seen. His green cloak accentuated his eyes, and his eyelashes moved like silk when he blinked. He could have been Joya with the green feathers that softly lay on top of his head, but the green goatee told me that he wasn't. Joya's only had feathers, not hair. A cross-breed, definitely; the same as his brother.

He was rather cute, but the feeling that engulfed my entire being drew me away from his facial features and directly to his eyes.

The Minions turned to look at me, their eyes not their own. There was something behind them, something I needed. I was drawn to all three of them. Not knowing which one to go to first, I slowly headed for Reso, as he was the closest. As if on cue, they all stood up, but I continued to walk to Reso and reached out to his face, my hunger beating inside me like jabbing fists.

Uncontrollably, I leaned forward, my lips close to his . . ..

A flicker of red came between us, and I blinked. Voice had jumped on the table and shoved Reso to the floor.

"Disconnect!" He was shouting. "Disconnect!"

Reso seemed confused, and Voice hit him across the face.

I screamed, horrified, and furious about his intrusion. I attacked him. He jumped aside and out of my reach, but I only wanted him away so that I could get to Reso.

"Reso! By The Name! Disconnect! Espy!" Voice shouted from across the room.

I knelt down toward Reso and stared into the black eyes that didn't contain him. Running my hand over the soft large ears on his head, I bent down towards his lips . . . and suddenly Reso was swept away from me, pulled across the floor by his feet by an invisible force. Screaming with fury, I whipped around to see Voice near the table again, and Espy was next to him. Their bodies shook as they held hands, commanding a power that took all of their strength and concentration.

Reso continued to slide across the floor, but he struggled against the mental force that pulled him to the wall. His body spun before he collided with it headfirst. He collapsed, unconscious.

With another scream, I snapped my head towards Voice and Espy, my eyes narrowing into slits. They both flew up and their clasped hands ripped apart as I sent them flying separately into the air and slamming into the wall. As they struggled to get up, I walked towards them, surging with power to do more damage. Instinct had overwhelmed me, and I wanted to destroy whatever had prohibited the satisfaction of my quenching.

"Stop, Jetticia! Please!" Voice scrambled to his feet, blood dripping from a gash on his head. "You don't know what you're doing!"

Clenching my teeth, I watched as Voice flew through the air again, hitting the other wall. I quickly turned my attention to Espy, who still sat on the floor, unable to get to his feet. As I stood over him, I watched him pause in his struggles and slowly lift his head to view my eyes.

"Jetticia . . .?"

I saw his plea, but I couldn't adhere to it. I wanted to hurt him; I wanted to tear him apart. I wanted to plunge the vastness of my anger into him, and one scream would discipline him to my liking.

I opened my mouth and inhaled the strength I needed to release on him and . . . something set my body on fire. I fell down on one knee and looked up to see Reso standing in the distance with an inactgun pointed in my direction. His feathers stood on end as he fired again, landing another paralyzing blow through my body, snapping the anger out of me. He fired a third time, slapping my back against the floor.

The last words I heard before falling to the floor were Espy's as he exclaimed, "By the Name . . .."

Chapter 11   Truth

I awoke, expecting to see my flesh rippling and inflamed, but I didn't feel a thing. I had been shot by an inactgun before, and I knew how I should feel now, but I didn't feel the pain. Thinking back, I had to convince myself that I did actually get shot, and three times at that. Didn't I?

I tried sitting up, but a pain in my head forced me back down. A flash of the Minions being flung against the wall entered my mind. I had felt such power, such enormous strength. By The Name, did I do that?

Suddenly, I began to hear whisperings in my head again, and I turned my attention to the door. The Minions entered with their hoods down. They looked wracked and upset; even their cloaks looked slightly rumpled. Yet I was stirred by their presence, my need awakening once again. I hungered.

Espy handed me a box and the scent of xaronae floated up from its closed lid. I wanted it, I wanted to tear open the box and gulp down every one, but I wouldn't. I couldn't. Once I ate, I would fall asleep and one of these cursed Minions would selfishly take me, and I would not know which one. No. No, not again.

I refused the box, but Espy laid it gently on my lap. "Please eat," he said.

I forced myself not to look at the box, not to hunger for it. Yet my body pained to be quenched. I pushed the box away.

Impatiently, Voice grabbed the box, opened its lid and stuffed the xaronae under my nose. I could smell its delicious scent.

"Eat!" he demanded.

Summoning up my will, I moved away, flinging a pillow in Voice's direction. If one of them was going to take me, then By the Name I would be awake to see it!

Pain shot through me and I moaned, grabbing myself around my stomach though it hurt everywhere.

Reso came to my side and knelt by the bed, taking my hand in both of his. Softly, almost desperately, he said, "He is coming."

"Reso!" Voice boomed as the box of xaronae shook in his hand.

Reso ignored his brother and gently stroked my hand. "This is absurd." I heard him say, but it was inside my mind. My mind! Telepathy?

It is not your place! You can't. . .. Voice mentally stormed, surprisingly unable to form words as his mind was filled with anger and uncertainty. *How dare you--*

He's here, Espy stated, walking towards the door.

Voice hesitated, obviously wanting to scold Reso more severely, but he was forced to exit quickly. Reso, patting my hand, followed his brothers out. I sat there puzzled, staring at the door that they had left open.

Looking down at the bed, I noticed the box of xaronae sitting at the end where Voice had dropped it. Slowly, I climbed out of the bed, my head swirling slightly when my feet touched the floor. I hung on to the bedpost to wait for the dizziness to pass. Once I was able, I walked to the end of the bed and closed my eyes, willing this new, whirling sensation to cease. Every movement made me dizzy.

When I opened my eyes, I felt that powerful pull again and my eyes lifted from the xaronae to see a large mass of darkness.

He stood in the middle of the room, his black cowl unmoving, but his presence made the air around him crackle.

Only his Wendh hands were visible, protruding from his long, wide sleeves. My eyes opened wide as shock hit me along with the rush of utter desire.

Ja'pah.

With wide strides, he crossed the expanse between us, stopping within inches of my breath. Bending down, his arms encircled my legs and waist, lifting me up from my feet, cradling me and placing me gently on the bed. Thick, black tentacles sprouted out from his sides, piercing through his cloak to writhe wildly in the air. Two of them surrounded my legs, spreading them wide with an aggressive yank, jerking my head back to the bed. The other two tentacles swarmed around my waist, pinning me down while his hands pulled on the body-piece Espy had given me. The garment slid from my body, ripping at one side, only to seal itself together again as he tossed it aside.

His claws grabbed my wrists and held them down above my head. I didn't have time to question. I didn't have time to think. I screamed as he thrust straight through me, slamming against that spot inside me with perfect accuracy. His flesh widened mine, filling me in utter completeness, pounding me with relentless satisfaction. I could only scream and moan with astonished pleasure.

His tentacles didn't allow me to move, squirm, or even to relieve just a bit of the intensity of his deep incisions.

The pleasure was beyond normal limits, beyond anything I had ever experienced. Too intense. I could only scream.

My last cry synchronized with the hot liquid that scorched my insides. I felt the pulsing of his flesh as he released, in crashing waves, the apex of his pleasure. Only then did his hands and black appendages release me and retract into his body, and he sat back on his knees.

My body flew about, my feet and hands kicking and punching the bed as it went through a violent spasm. He watched silently as I convulsed, my body forcing itself to relax, and then reverting to sudden twitches. I could only move my eyes when it was over, as the rest of my body wouldn't respond. My throat was swollen and numb from screaming; I couldn't utter a sound. Filled with fear, extreme awe and pleasure, I couldn't have spoken anyway.

He reached down and slowly touched my cheek, filling me with a hot, soothing sensation. His hand moved down to my neck, my shoulder, down to my breast where he lingered, circling his fingertip around my hardened nipple, sending tingling ripples from its tip down the rest of my body. He leaned forward as the darkness inside the hood hovered close to my face, and he entered me again.

There was no fumbling, no resistance, just precise, rigid flesh penetrating me with unerring aim. I gasped and exhaled airily in unison with his thrusts. He took longer but was gentler than he was during the first delicious course. He allowed me to move, to pull back slightly when it became too much for me. When he finally released me again, he lingered inside me for a moment and pulled my head to the side.

I went stiff with the knowledge of what he was about to do next as he exposed my neck. My body trembled, though I didn't know if it was from my anxious expectations or from the sensations he filled me with.

I felt his lips, his kiss, and then the pain as his teeth sank into my flesh. The pain didn't last long as it was replaced with a blissful surge that swept through my body. I listened to him suck and felt him dig his teeth deeper to produce more warm thickness onto his wet tongue. When he had his fill, he expelled his blood into me with his teeth, sending an electric charge throughout my body. Once completed, he licked my neck, his saliva stanching the drench of blood and immediately healing the wound.

He leaned back, allowing me to stare into the blackness in his hood, and then I felt something warm on my lips. Looking down, I saw him holding xaronae, gently pushing it against my mouth. I opened my mouth involuntarily and allowed him to place the delicacy inside. When it melted, the warm juices soothed the rawness of my throat. I trembled slightly for a moment as he placed another xaronae on my lips, knowing now why I had so craved the small delicacy, knowing now that each sweet morsel contained his Wendh blood.

He fed them to me as if daring me to decline. Taking his time, he placed each one on my lips, inspecting me carefully as I sucked and swallowed every one of them. Watching me consume his blood excited him; it excited every Wendh, and his hardness moved into me again. He pulled my hair as he licked my neck, and I moaned with pleasure and reveled in his dominance. He surged, but this time with a throaty growl, the only sound I had ever heard him make, and then darkness flooded my eyes, blinding me suddenly. When I blinked, I could see again, but he had disappeared.

I moved my head to the side and looked around the room. He wasn't there. I turned to the other side, but it was empty as well. I felt a tear slide down my cheek. Parts of my body were in so much in pain, while other parts felt pleasurably soothing. I lay there in an uncomfortable position, unable to actually turn my whole body, and stared at a spot on the wall.

# # #

Three days passed before someone finally came to my room. Reso found me sitting on the sofa, staring at nothing. I had been that way since the Ja'pah had taken me. I blindly sat and watched the holoscreen, ate without tasting, and slept without feeling its relaxation. My mind was mostly blank, unable to think but of one question.

Reso sat next to me without saying a word. I almost didn't notice him. Yet his presence there brought me back to reality, and I mouthed the words, the question, that had lingered in my head for days. He wasn't facing me, so he didn't see my question. Swallowing, I tried again to force sound from my throat. I asked again.

" . . . Why?"

His blue hood turned in my direction, but he did not answer.

Determination, the first feeling I had felt in days, made me ask again. "What does this mean?"

His hood tilted down in shame, swaying for a moment before turning and answering, "I told Voice that this was absurd." He then lifted his hood, as if forcing himself to look at me. "I told the Ja'pah. They should have known you were going to outgrow us, that we wouldn't be able to restrain your power, your strength, the union, as long as it kept going forward. But they were afraid that someone would find out, and they would target you, and they would kill our Ja'pah by killing you."

I stared at him, blinking. He had said more than I have ever heard him say, and yet I couldn't respond.

"He told us to handle you," his soft voice was pleading for my comprehension, "for all three of us to handle you, but we couldn't. I tried to tell him, but he wouldn't listen. He wanted to keep you here where no one would know, where no one would find out. It was absurd. You were becoming too violent, too unstable. I tried to tell them; I showed them the vase."

I looked at him, suddenly enlightened.

"It was the first sign of your strength, and then you made me trip in the hallway, which only confirmed it. We had to do something with you to distract you. I finally convinced the Ja'pah to train you, to make everyone believe that you were just a Minion. He finally agreed, reluctantly. And then he still wanted us to control you. If he had done it, if he had held you mentally secure, then you would have sensed him, and you would have found out what he was to you. So, it was up to us, but your senses were growing too strong for us to mute. Trying to control that was absurd. Voice thought that if you didn't know, and if someone had targeted you, the Ja'pah would be safe, because you would contain no knowledge of who he was to you."

I continued to stare at him as he paused.

"Stupidity," Reso hissed. "You were finding out every day. They should have known it wouldn't last long. They should have known that you couldn't stop The Calling."

Slowly, I turned my head away from him. I should have laughed at him like I did with Tokie and deny everything that he had just said, but I couldn't.

"I'm Wendh," I mumbled. "Wendhs don't mate with Wendhs." But I knew that was a lie. It happened on my home planet all the time. My father was a product of that kind of mating, and his father before him. But I wasn't, yet my relatives were. Did that affect me somehow? Was it my father's planet's way of joining that caused this? Was it because he did not allow the full metamorphosis of my mother to be complete?

"I'm *not* Wendh," I said. That was the only reasonable explanation. "But I'm not Human. I'm a different species."

"Of course you're Wendh," Reso whispered, "and Human. You're the only kind of mixture that could mate with the Ja'pah."

I disagreed. "The Ja'pah is Wendh. Wendhs don't mate with Wendhs." But more importantly, "Wendhs don't have The Calling for other Wendhs!"

"But you had The Calling," he said softly. "You had it."

I stuttered slightly and then closed my mouth. I couldn't object. He was right. I did follow my hunger, and the Ja'pah must have been the Being whom I was following. He was with all three Minions at every location, and they intervened each time I tried to come near him. But . . . "Did he not have The Calling?"

"No," Reso said plainly.

"Why?"

He shifted slightly on the sofa. "He wasn't listening."

That didn't make sense. A Wendh didn't have a choice but to listen. How could one choose not to listen to Suphyz?

"The doctors told you I was in Calling. The Hyperian."

"Yes."

"And you knew who I had come for?"

"Not at first. We tested it when you were asleep. We each walked up to you and you didn't respond. When he entered the room, you tried to wake yourself. And he also sensed something, but he wouldn't acknowledge it. It took us some time to convince him what was happening. Only when his hunger was not being quenched by others . . . .." He trailed off and started again. "The night you attacked us, he saw you through Espy's eyes and stopped everything to get to you, unreasonably using Espy's body."

I smiled slightly. "I was beginning to believe it was Espy."

"No. We . . ." it was hard for him to speak his next words. "We . . . we are all attracted to you."

I gawked and he quickly added, "Only because of the Ja'pah's link to you, you understand. If he had just relinquished our duty, our connection to you, we wouldn't have felt this way!"

"Now," I breathed, "now I know your secret, Reso. What other duties do you have regarding me?"

Reso remained silent. There was more? I wasn't serious about my last question, but his reaction told me that there was indeed more. And, of course whatever the "other duties" were, he wouldn't tell me explicitly. Of course. He was a Minion, after all. They were full of secrets. I had to figure them out myself.

"When you are ready," he said, standing up to leave, "please meet me in the training room."

I watched him quickly leave and continued to sit there looking towards the doorway. So, it was back to training as if nothing had happened, as if I hadn't been ravished by the imperial of the Underworld, as if I weren't the mate of the Ja'pah. The idea still stunned and frightened me. Me, a True Mate of a Wendh, a mate of the Ja'pah. Why would Suphyz make such a decision? Why me? I was much too blemished to be with such a male.

Yet I had been blessed.

I looked towards the end of the couch and concentrated. A pillow jerked. I tried again, and this time it lifted into the air. I held it still before floating it back down on the sofa. I could hardly breathe as the release of the cycles of sadness of not being completely Wendh overwhelmed me.

Telekinesis.

The power was dithering.

I couldn't help it. I made the pillow float again, and then again, zooming across the room, zipping and soaring, until a slight queasiness made me stop. I was doing too much, too fast. I needed practice, and my mind needed to strengthen.

But I had it. Telekinesis. Telepathy. Tele-. Tele-. Tele-. I had them all!

I had heard the Minions' whisperings. I had mentally heard their voices. I made that pillow float. I made that vase crash. I made a Minion stumble.

Unexpected tears swept over me, filling me with such joy, yet uneasiness. Ja'pah. He ruled the Underworld where crime, hatred, death, and murder dwelled at its peak. I was only a thief, but I really didn't expect to stay that way, did I? Had this always been my path, to lead me here? Was this the life I was supposed to lead to be truly Wendh?

With every drop of his blood, my Human side was diminishing. Mating with the Ja'pah would probably not take one or two cycles for the metamorphosis to be complete, as I was already half Wendh, but with the rate that he was going, with mere drops of his blood in sweets, it might just take that long. I had heard that the Ja'pah took his time with everything.

Ja'pah, my True Mate--the thought of him taking me made me shiver with both expectation and apprehension. Ja'pah. His name sounded so sweet on my lips, yet it also made my heart beat with fear. Who was . . .?

Wait. Who. Who?

Was that it? Was that the secret that the Minions possessed? Was it his identity? Did they struggle to keep his identity from me? By the Name!

Wendh mating was a complete connection: physically, spiritually and mentally. And because my Human side was changing, the Ja'pah's blood should be making my connection to him, learning his entire being through dreaming or by instinctual knowledge. Did they suppress my dreams, my innate knowledge? Had I dreamt of the Ja'pah's past, of his ancestors, without knowing it? When was the last time I had dreamed? I didn't remember. I didn't know. By the Name, they controlled my mind!

I jumped up and ran out of the room and down the hall. I flew to the training room where Reso waited for me, ready to begin his dance.

"The Ja'pah . . . ," I said, out of breath. "I do not dream."

Reso paused before standing straight up. "You must not speak of this."

"I should know, shouldn't I? I do know."

Hush, child! the words rang through my head. *Do not speak of this!*

For the first time, I mentally spoke to another Being--my first mental words. *I do know, don't I?*

When Reso mentally responded, I didn't know whether to leap from excitement or bash his face in for changing the subject.

Follow my movements, he commanded, and began to wave his arms in the air.

I paused, hoping he would give in, but he continued his physical training. Reluctantly, I dropped the question, but the thought brooded in my mind. I knew who the Ja'pah was, but I did not know. What was he? Who was he? And why did such knowledge reign down on me?

Shaking my head, I followed Reso's movements, knowing that the dance would calm and bring order to my mind. Still my thoughts rambled on, going from one to the next until they returned to the Wendh abilities I had inherited.

I tested my mental communication on Reso and began asking about my movements while we trained. Though Reso was quiet in nature and resistant to answer, from time to time he would mentally project what I was doing wrong. And each time he replied, my moves, my insides would dance with elation.

Telepathy!

I thought of my parents, my sister, my brother, my grandparents. What conversations could I be engage in now? What mental pictures could they send to me so that I could clearly understand the stories that they told around the dinner table? What images could I broadcast to them of my travels among the stars!

And the Ja'pah. My True Mate. I could tell them--

I quickly wiped the thought from my mind as reality swept in, knowing the Ja'pah's identity could be my death, and his. I was in a dangerous situation, and the path I was set upon was too treacherous even for my family. They could never know what blood was coursing through my veins; no one could.

The realization was disheartening, yet I knew what I had decided was right. I couldn't return home. I couldn't leave the Minions' side. I couldn't expose what I was to anyone.

So this was what the Goddess Suphyz had planned for me. All this time, while I was silently cursing Her name, hating my own existence, believing I was something abnormal, She had this plan.

Oh, Suphyz, how could I have ever doubted You? Please forgive this faithless disciple. Please forgive my stupid ignorance. I should have trusted You. I should have known my life was important, that You did not make something exist unless it was important.

Yet . . . the Ja'pah? My True Mate? That understanding made me tremble.

By the Name, Suphyz, what game have You constructed here?

Chapter 12   Jancso

Several days and trainings later, Reso told me to shower and shockingly ordered me put on my white cowl and meet him in the landing bay. I did as I was told, knowing that this meant we were departing and feeling grateful for leaving the meteoroid for a while. The flight destination was to Jancso, Isdol's rival planet, where I had unexpectedly run into Voice and Espy, thanks to Tokie.

Tokie. I had almost forgotten about her. I wondered where she was now, though she was most likely home. It was better that she was no longer around me, especially with what had happened. Though she held secrets beyond secrets, I didn't know what she would do with the knowledge that I was the Ja'pah's True Mate.

My mind quickly turned away from thoughts of Tokie as Jancso's buildings again caught my eye. They were more colorful than I remembered, and the streamers and laser lights were much brighter. Beings danced in the street and sang songs while a large holoscreen displayed the child image of Imperial TeNeil's youngest son before he was kidnapped during the Xarthren wars. The image wasn't even accurate. The royal child was at least ten cycles old before he was killed, yet the image that was displayed and produced on all the good luck charms showed him four cycles younger. Ten cycles was still very young for a Wendh, but six cycles made a better impression on the Four Quadrants.

Politics. Using the death of a child for public image, and the child was strange and deformed at that!

LaSar was his name. He had born a hundred-and-four cycles earlier. He was supposed to have been some kind of celestial Being because he had wings, or something. Never had a Wendh been born with wings, so of course, he must have been a sign from Suphyz Herself. He was going to deliver us to a new world, a new age, that Charmed One. But the only change that occurred during his era was to get himself captured and killed during the first cycle of the war.

His death did bring up the spirits of the Four Quadrants, though, and together, for the next four cycles, they drove the Xarthrens back to their part of the universe. LaSar became the symbol of our victory and a reminder of the bloodshed during the war. He also reminded the Imperial's subjects that their ruler was just as vulnerable and common as any sentient Being, for he also had suffered losses to the Xarthrens. It kept him in reign and in good spirits with his supporters.

Wait. The Seven Days Fest. Had it been a whole cycle already?

It was this time just one cycle ago when I had searched out the Reuss to find Vrang to quench my hunger and was forced to be a part of Vrang's cate. I stared up at the royal child's multiple projections plastered in a circle, forming a frame as we flew inside the two-seat galer in silence. An entire cycle had come and gone, and this was where I ended up.

The galer rounded several buildings before entering a dark alley and then plunging straight down to the ground. I gasped, holding my breath, thinking perhaps the galer had malfunctioned, but I didn't feel resistance as we were immediately surrounded in darkness, still flying. We were in the dark for several minutes before I saw speckles of light, and then florescent walls and tunnels. I sat, flabbergasted, eying this new world--an underground dark city quite different from the colorful one above.

"Don't look too surprised," Espy joked. "Every planet has it's Quuto."

"This is unlawful ground?" I stared at the many flyers that shot past us.

"You know what our lives are, Jetticia, where our cates are," Reso answered.

Of course I did. I wasn't naive. I looked out the window again and watched the speedy movements inside the connecting tunnels webbed across the buildings. Inside them were skitters and linked vehicles with compartments that transported passengers. Buildings surged out of the underground rocks, which were the only things supporting them besides a few tunnels used as beams that shot down and were embedded in the rock below.

"So what's this cate?" I asked, turning away from the scene outside. I shouldn't bother with questions because I never got a direct answer anyway, but amazingly, Reso responded.

"We have to pick up something."

The galer tilted as we zoomed inside a building. We landed in a fairly occupied terminal, which slightly confused me, because I thought we were supposed to be covert. Reso stood up to leave, and I received no lecture before the galer's doors opened; however, my experience told me to follow whatever Reso said and did.

As we went through the terminal, Beings stared at us with awe and whispered, which made me smile and imagine what they thought. A new Ja'pah Minion? When did *he* come about?

"Espy, I am so honored to see you again," a female Yetanlier, or Natanlier, said as she stood in front of us. She had oiled her green scales, and her circular lips poked out as if wanting to give Espy a kiss.

"Maheir Savva," Espy nodded to her with utter respect. "I am always pleased."

She smiled, displaying her white pointed teeth, and then turned her attention to me. "You bring a new companion."

"Senses," Espy introduced me, as I wonder if he just made up that name. "My sister."

"Sister? Female?" Savva's interest was piqued. "I didn't know you had a sister."

"She is sister to all three of us."

She smiled with understanding. "I see." Her brown eyes appraised me, and then gesturing behind her, she quickly said, "Come, then. Your package is waiting."

We followed her through tunnels limited to Beings who looked high-caste and probably were. There was security at every corner and floaters monitoring the hallways. I immediately defined this place as a storehouse containing very valuable items, and I wondered if the Reuss knew of this place.

"It's been almost a cycle," Savva was saying to Reso, as I walked behind him.

"I have been quite busy," he politely answered.

"I hope you are not too busy," Savva hinted, giving him a slight glance back.

"At the moment, I am," Reso replied, "but in a few months, I will not be as occupied."

I swallowed a laugh and wondered if they actually had sexual encounters or if Savva was simply a very determined female.

We stopped in front of what appeared to be a wall. Reso held out his hand, and a door glittered into view. Savva bowed to Reso with a graceful sweep, gave me another look and walked slowly down the hall. Reso didn't open the door until she had rounded the corner. He stared at the corner wall for some time, perhaps watching her with those penetrating eyes. When he was satisfied, he pressed his palm on the door and we stepped through.

A black cylinder, larger than myself, stood in the middle of the small room. It was the only object in sight. Reso quickly went to it, tapped on the controls on its side panel and examined some numbers on a screen. He nodded his approval to me and then stood in front of the cylinder and waited.

I wanted to ask what was going on but kept silent as we stood there for more than an hour. I knew Reso preferred silence, even mentally. Suddenly, a light appeared above us and shone on the black container. Reso waved to me to come to him and then gripped the sides of the container, and I did the same. We were lifted into the air and shot down a tunnel so fast that I could barely hang on.

"Steic!" I shouted, wishing Reso had warned me before we went flying through the air like a laser beam.

Before I knew it, we were out in the open again, and in a quick blink, a flash of bright light washed over us and we were falling to the floor of a red-lit room. The cylinder dropped with only a slight thud as Reso and I landed with a tumble and then on our feet.

I felt woozy. I didn't mind fast rides, but when they came with sudden jerks, especially through portals, it made me sick.

"Are you alright?" Reso came to me as I bent over, trying not to vomit.

"No, I'm not alright!" I glared at him, which I'm sure he could see, despite the darkness of my hood. "Why can't you just explain what we're about to do before we do it?"

Another voice announced, "Then it wouldn't be any fun, now would it?"

Voice stood with his left hand outstretched in front of my face. A small pill sat in his palm. I grabbed it out of his hand and popped it in my mouth. Immediately, the wooziness was gone. When I straightened up, Voice was smiling back a laugh.

I frowned at him. "This isn't funny." I would have stormed out of the room if I had known where I was, but then again, that would jeopardize the cate. But, wait. How did he know that would make me sick? What made me more sick was how much more they knew about me. Fleiking Minions!

"He's doing well," Reso interrupted, patting the side of the cylinder. "I only hope his hunger is still at its beginning stages like we found him."

"It should be," Voice said confidently. "I'll escort Senses to Espy, while you take care of our friend here."

Who? What? There's someone inside this thing?

Answers would have to come at a later time, I knew, as Voice looked like he was ready to leave. The cate wasn't over yet. Voice extended his hand to me, and I ignored it. With a shrug, he exited the room, and I begrudgingly followed.

To my surprise, we were in the basement of a building, though I had thought at first we were in another ship. I strutted behind Voice, who walked quickly down empty halls and up a long escalator where, the closer we got to the next level, the more voices I heard.

We stepped out to the ground floor of a hotel. Residents filled the crowded lounge--too many bodies--which told me that the hotel was not very expensive. We made our way through the mass and I watched the signs to figure out our destination. I heard several whispers directed our way as we headed for the hotel's terminal, boarded Voice's ship and left Jancso.

"Such impoliteness," Voice teased me as I sat next to him in complete silence with folded arms, filled with resentment.

"I wouldn't be so impolite if you Minions were more structured."

"Like the Reuss?" Voice said with amusement, baring his perfect teeth as he grinned.

I sat up. "Exactly like the Reuss and every other cate I've been on! There were directions and instructions!"

"And sloppy cates."

I hissed at him. "Little do you know."

"I actually know quite a lot," he smugly said.

I leaned forward as I spoke my next few words, making sure he heard each one. "If you know so much, then why didn't you know that the three of you couldn't restrain me indefinitely?"

The ends of his mouth dropped, erasing his flawless smile. He said nothing. I had hit a delicate subject, and he wasn't going to dwell on it.

I smiled in my victory.

# # #

Voice's ship met Espy's in the middle of nowhere, hours later. As we boarded, I thought of the lack of sleep I had endured.

Careful, Voice mentally warned his brother, *she's in one of those moods*.

"I heard that!" I spat, but inwardly smiled for being able to mentally hear their teasing.

Voice gleefully disembarked and left Espy to attend to me.

It was the first time that Espy and I were alone together since he had knocked me unconscious. He was uneasy and barely looked at me, and I didn't know what to say.

I thought of something that might be funny. "You give quite a blow, Espy."

He remained silent at the controls, his hood shifting slightly in my direction before turning straight ahead again.

I tried again. "I didn't know you could be as quiet as Reso."

He laughed then, a sudden laugh that startled me. "Neither did I."

We fell silent again and I spoke up. "So . . . what's the cate this time?"

He paused before answering, "We'll have to wait before continuing."

"Where are we waiting?"

"On Isdol."

My mind spun with possible conclusions. "Isdol? I heard you speaking of Vortsi to your brothers at the home base, and Reso convinced you two to go to Isdol in his place. But Vortsi is missing. I heard about it on the Unicom and . . .. you know where he is, don't you?"

Espy didn't answer, but I knew I was close to something.

"What is it that Vortsi needs to do on Isdol, and what does this have to do with The Lady's kidnapping by the Reuss?"

Before Espy could answer, I felt a darkness sweep over him that made my heart jump. It quickly left and he turned to me.

"Come with me," he said, leaving the controls of the ship on autopilot and escorting me to the back.

He stepped to the side after palming a door's panel, allowing me to enter the room first. The door shut immediately with no Espy behind me. When would I learn?

I opened my mouth to shout obscenities at the door, knowing he had probably locked me in the room because I was asking too many questions, but most likely because I was getting too close to the truth of this cate. The first sound of curses stopped in the middle of my throat as I felt someone else in the room.

I turned around slowly, suddenly noticing the small amount of light that filled the room. Surrounded by shadows, he stepped out, his cloak moving without pattern, his hood covering unknown blackness. As he came closer, I took steps backwards until my back hit the locked door.

My mind wouldn't focus on words or images as I numbly stared at the approaching Ja'pah. He stopped before me, his hood staring down at me. I hadn't realized before how tall he was, but I could now see that the top of my head only reached the edge of his shoulders.

He reached outward, both arms caging me, as his palms pressed against the door. I dared to look up at him, trying to see behind the darkness of his hood, but failing.

His tentacles sprouted out and waved in the air, bringing me out of my stupor. Something was odd about them. Something . . . six? There were six of them; he had six tentacles! Why did I not see that before? Six! No Wendh had six tentacles. By The Name, he wasn't a full Wendh!

All six swarmed around me, picking me up from my feet, holding me up against the door as if I were sitting in a lifted chair. The Ja'pah parted my legs, and as soon as I knew what he wanted, I became nervous. I wasn't in hunger; I was not filled with passion yet. But as soon as he began to part my white cloak and mentally tug at the fitted undergarment, which came loose at the seams and dropped to the floor, my insides began to warm.

His head bent down to my neck, sending chills through me as he kissed and nibbled on sensitive areas. He widened my legs a bit more and took a step forward between them. His hand immediately grabbed my upper arms, pinning them to the door as I felt his flesh at the tip of me. He growled deeply as his fleshy staff pushed itself inside, hidden behind the darkness of his cloak and the closeness of our bodies.

I jerked from the sensitivity, and jerked again as he moved deeper. The jerking slowly ebbed away, replaced with wide-eyed moans. My head accidentally hit the door as my body went wild with the sensation. The Ja'pah lifted me from the door, carried me across the room and slammed me on a table. At the same time, his flesh remained deep inside.

I arched up, screaming to relieve some of the sensation that warned to overwhelm me, but that only caused him to thrust harder, drilling me until unintelligible syllables escaped my lips.

Ahhhhheeeeiiiiuhhhh!

As hard flesh tore into soft flesh, screams and moans blurred together as my body fought for release, but the pleasuring torture continued on and on and on.

Finally, a surge of hot flood exploded just as I was becoming exhausted. He withdrew himself and hovered over me, watching as I caught my breath. Gently, he touched my cheek with his fingertip and lingered there for a few moments before moving away from me. His sudden lift made me blink as he headed to the door, his cloak snapping the air.

"No more questions," his voice rumbled as the door slid open and he stepped through it.

My head hit the table as I let out my breath.

When I had recovered enough to climb down from the table and re-dress, I gathered enough courage to leave the room to find Espy and possibly the Ja'pah. I was slightly saddened to find out that my True Mate was no longer on the ship and sat quietly next to Espy, my mind filled with the Ja'pah and his touch.

I closed my eyes, still feeling the waves of his pleasure and his skin wrapped around me. Six tentacles. Could this Being truly be my True Mate? Such pleasure would make me an addict for sure.

My mind took a sudden turn as I thought about his tentacles. Six! Six tentacles! He couldn't be Wendh. That explained everything. That explained my Calling for him, and Espy did say the Ja'pah didn't hear The Calling because he wasn't listening. That's what all high-caste Wendhs say about other species who don't receive The Calling; that they weren't listening.

The Ja'pah wasn't Wendh, but I was. That made sense. Yet, the Minions suppressed my dreams, which only non-Wendhs had; however, I had the Calling. Were we both not Wendhs, yet were? Were we both cross-species? If he wasn't Wendh, then what was he? What kind of Being has six tentacles?

I turned and looked at Espy, but the Ja'pah's words rang through my mind. No more questions, he had said. Thinking of his voice sent chills over my skin. So deep, so penetrating, so wonderful.

So perfect.

"Jetta." Espy distracted me. No; *he* was behind Espy's eyes.

I sat up and looked at Espy, knowing the Ja'pah was inside him.

"Be careful for me."

I stared into Espy's green eyes, seeing the dark shadow lingering behind them, and then, with a mental wisp, it was gone.

Espy blinked, a bit shocked that I was so near his face. I backed away, embarrassed. "Sorry," I mumbled.

Espy didn't answer.

Chapter 13   Isdol

The weeks on Isdol were disconcerting. Here I was, I Wendh, among billions of Wendh-haters. I was grateful for my cowl, which blended in nicely with all the whiteness on the planet.

Every building, every piece of furniture, every inanimate object was white. White for purity; purity from Wendhs. Their pride for being so pure, for never allowing Wendhs to mate with their species, showed in everything on the planet. It took us three days to get through Customs (a process no other planet had) to be admitted on the planet, being that we were Minions of a Wendh.

And then we waited.

Days turned to weeks while we sat in a white comfortable hotel, went out occasionally to eat on white plates, and did some minor trading in the unlawful white grounds of Isdol, shipping large crates off the planet.

"Priceless statues and rare delicacies," Espy explained as Customs checked the crates. The personnel were quite familiar with Espy's cargo, as he had been doing this kind of trading for cycles on this planet. They leisurely looked over the items and gave the order to allow them off the planet.

Every planet sold their rarities to high bidders, and only the very smart and well known were allowed in that kind of business. The Ja'pah was one of them.

So, we continued buying and selling for weeks on end. When the day finally arrived, I had no knowledge of it. We attended a grand ball, which was nothing unusual, as Isdol seemed to have a grand ball every other week. I had seen The Lady herself at a few of them. She was also going to attend this particular ball, but not many Beings knew about it.

We were usually given an isolated booth in the rear, but this night we were closer to the entertainment. The dancers were just a step down from us, and the orchestra was five tables away. I was beginning to wonder why we were given such good seating when I looked around and noticed not that many people had attended this ball. The booths from the third level and above were all empty.

The dancers began to perform more frantically, getting everyone's attention as they changed outfits and colors. It was a relief to see something other than white. I had begun staring at my food every time I ate just to see some color. These dancers, with the white room for a background, were the most wonderful sight I had seen in cycles, I thought, and the colors were almost inebriating.

One of the dancers approached me, waving her long flowing red cloth in the air, allowing it to flutter behind her. Her hair was also red, accenting her brilliant green eyes. She smiled and winked at me, and I stopped myself from shuffling in my chair. She probably thought I was male. She lingered by our table for a while, flirtatiously dancing, flinging her red cloth over her head and around her body before again rejoining her group.

Seems like you made a friend, Espy mentally teased.

I thought the word passed faster than this, Espy, I thought back to him. *Don't they know I'm Senses, a sister, not a brother?*

Espy answered with a mental laugh.

The Lady made her grand entrance as everyone fluttered around for her attention. She was actually quite attractive. Her fine, green hair was pinned up, with trails of curls flowing down her back, and her nails were painted green, which made her white hands appear even whiter. She wore her traditional pantsuit that bellowed out at the hems, and gems sparkled around her neck that seemed to equal jewelry worn by the Imperial's mate herself.

Every eye was on The Lady of Isdol, even when she ate. Some eyes darted between her and her brother, Torshincal, and their dazzling cousin, Yolikeg, whose outfits always seemed to be grander than The Lady's. Bodyguards stood by all three of them, keenly aware of everything that went on in the room.

The royal three's time was short in the ballroom, and they soon exited as quickly as they had appeared. I looked at Espy for some sign of leaving as well, but he gave none. We stayed until the dancers and orchestra had cleaned up and left the building.

I thought we were heading back to our hotel, but we ended up in the unlawful area of Isdol instead and flew to an unused plot of land. We exited the two-seat galer and found a door in the ground. Espy lifted it with his mind and jumped down inside.

"Float down," he mentally beckoned me.

Float? What? *Float?* I thought back to him. *I've never--*

You're wasting time, now float!

I looked around as if someone could help, or stop me, from attempting something that could possibly kill me. I didn't know how deep the hole was, but I didn't have a choice. Fleiking, unstable Minions. In all my training, not once did I mentally command my own body. Knowing there wasn't anyone to aid me and also that cates come before self, I jumped down, trying to mentally see myself floating.

It didn't work.

I was falling too fast, and I lost my concentration. Something grabbed me, and I was gently lowered until I found solid footing.

"Almost," he said with encouragement. "Come on."

We walked underground in darkness. Even the color black appealed to me after the endless white. Then the black changed color, to a strange gray, and the strangeness of the light made me pause. My eyes focused, and I could see. I could see in the dark!

The Ja'pah blood? Of course it was. It took a moment for it to take effect, and then I could see as if it were day.

I followed Espy in amazement, looking at every crack and spec of dirt around me, and then I was hit by filth and smothering air. These were forgotten sewage tunnels, or, more likely, substitute routes for waste, if needed. The latter seemed more likely because of the smell. I covered my nose. Along with enhanced eyesight, I received the keen smell as well, and we were traveling deeper into the stench.

We walked until my legs were numb from pain and I could think of nothing else but keeping one foot in front of the other. Espy finally allowed us to rest, and we sat in a tunnel too narrow for us to sit across from each other. I fell asleep immediately, only to be nudged awake at what seemed like just a few minutes later. We continued our hike.

Soon, we came to a ladder where we stopped. It didn't appear to be any different than the many we had already passed, but this one began our ascent. The climb was worse than the walking. We would climb to a level, walk for a few hours and then climb some more. Finally, we stopped by what looked like an energy barrier that had been sitting there for cycles. Espy reached into his cloak and pulled out something that glowed.

We'll both jump through when I say, he mentally said and paused a few moments before commanding, "Go."

He didn't give me time to prepare as the tool temporarily opened a large hole and we jumped through. We came to several more barriers like this with only a few seconds to give us time to cross.

At a some of the barriers, Espy stopped and waited, giving us time to rest, so I thought, but he was staring at the glowing object in his hand. I looked at it too, but saw nothing. It must have been timed to work at certain intervals, perhaps so that those monitoring the barriers wouldn't be paying attention to it when we interrupted the energy flow.

We finally came to a wall where Espy stopped and stared. I wondered what he saw behind its thickness and waited for his command.

"Her name is Dalaen," Espy suddenly said. "She's a personal servant of important guests that come to this house."

I didn't know what he was talking about, but I listened and memorized his words.

"Go left from the exit; take the hall until you see a picture that projects mists from its scenery of waterfalls. Go left again, and then make a right. You'll come to an elevator. Speak into it saying, 'maquef,' and take it until it stops. Turn right when the door opens and walk to the guards. Stay there until ordered otherwise."

Espy didn't ask me if I understood everything, but I didn't think he had time to ask. He waved his hand over the wall until it rippled and bubbled, and we walked through it.

I suddenly heard grunting and moaning. Looking around, I realized we were in a bathroom that had recently been used. Espy rushed through, heading to the door and I quickly followed.

We walked through a small living quarters to a bedroom where a large man and petite female were aggressively joining. They didn't notice the two strangers in the bedroom, nor did they seem to know how sleepy they were becoming in the middle of their lovemaking. Espy waved his hand, which held a small device that sprayed invisible mist, and the two lovers suddenly slumped on the bed.

"Go back to the shower and bathe quickly."

I ran back to the bathroom, turned on the water, took off my cloak and washed the filth from my body. I held my cloak out as well, allowing the substances in the water to clean it. Before I could dry myself, Espy was in the bathroom, holding out a small can.

"Spray this on."

I took the can, spraying every inch of my body, a gesture I knew very well how to do. This was some sort of utiq oil, but it dried much more quickly than the oil I was used to. I didn't have time to inspect myself, nor would I have used Bymé to activate any of the computer devices in the room--that could be traced. I assumed I must have been transformed into Dalaen, who had just been put to sleep underneath her lover.

Espy handed me some clothes, stuck something on my neck and took my cloak. "Go. I'll clean up here."

As soon as I dressed, I exited from the small apartment and immediately ran into Isdollem guards patrolling the hallway. I stepped back, almost with fear, until one of the guards sent a quick smile my way before continuing on. This Dalaen must be a female who gets around. The male sleeping in the room just might be a guard as well.

I made a conscious effort to return my heartbeat to normal and turned left. Espy's directions weren't as clear as they had seemed. The hallway turned and branched off, and I wasn't sure if I was continuing straight or not. Finally, I found the picture with the waterfall and turned left. There was an immediate branch and I turned right.

More guards. They lined the entire hallway. I hesitated, thinking one of them would ask me for my identity, but none of them did as I walked by. To stay in character, I smiled at a few of them, and one actually blushed. Reaching the elevator, I said the command, but the door didn't open.

"Maquef," I repeated, more anxious now, and I fondled with the voice modulator hidden under my collar that Espy had stuck on my neck.

A guard approached me. "Dalaen. Did you forget again?" His voice was not friendly.

I opened my mouth but shut it again, and gave him an innocent shrug with a sly smile.

"This is the last time," he reprimanded. "Next time I'll report you. Maques," he said to the door, and it opened immediately.

I stepped through and dared to look up at the guard who stared at me with slight suspicion.

"I won't forget next time," I suddenly said, feeling that I should say something.

"You say that every time," he grumbled and turned his back as the door began to close.

I continued smiling, playing my role. I didn't want to seem too relieved just in case unseen cameras were watching me as the elevator's doors closed. The elevator went up, and up, with no indicator of how many floors, but from the length of the ride, it was quite a way.

When the door opened, I found myself face-to-face with two guards. My heart jumped, thinking they were there to apprehend me, but then I saw the grand door only a few steps behind them to the right. I smiled at them, though they did not respond, before passing between them and going to the door.

I waited, as instructed, not moving until I heard from Espy. One of the guards turned to look at me and frowned. I gave him another smile, but he walked up to me and grabbed me by the wrist.

"What's wrong, Dalaen?"

I quickly answered. "Nothing."

"Then why are you just standing there?"

My mind spun. *Espy, please hurry!*

The second guard turned around.

"I . . ." I stumbled. "I forgot my code again."

"Code?"

Immediately, I knew that was the wrong answer and tried to cover it up. "At the elevator. I forgot it."

He didn't believe me. He released me and then activated his qCarpus on his wrist to most likely investigate my presence there. With a quick motion, I grabbed his arm and twisted it. Twirling around him, I used him as a shield from the weapon fired by the second guard. But that guard was already on the ground, and the guard I stood behind fell limp and went down as well.

I turned around, seeing the grand doors wide open and an armed guard putting his weapon away. He had something poking from his nose.

"Put these in," he shouted, tossing something at me.

I caught it in the air and recognized them as the same plugs that were in his nose. I immediately began to feel sleepy. Slowly, I placed one in my nose and felt a surge jerk me awake. I put the other one in.

The guard ran back inside the room, and I followed. Guards within the room were slumped down on the floor, and I had to jump over some of them to keep up with my new partner. The room was quite lavish, even though I caught just blurs of it from my peripheral vision. We ran into a bedroom where a guard lay bleeding on the floor; it appeared that he had been shot several times. A female was slumped on the bed.

"Pick her up," the guard ordered as I wondered why this male was shot while the other guards were affected by the gas.

Something was wrong.

"Pick her up!" the guard repeated, glancing back at the entrance.

I went to the female and turned her over.

The Lady.

The shock made me hesitate.

"Hurry!" The guard shouted, "We're blocked! All sides are blocked! We only have one way out!"

I tried lifting the sleeping female, but she was too heavy.

"What are you doing?"

I stared back at the anxious guard and then looked back down at The Lady. He wanted me to float her, but I didn't . . . I never--

He shouted again. "Hurry!"

His anxiety jerked me out of my hesitation, and I quickly thought back to when I made Reso trip in the hallway, the pillow lift off the couch, and the other small items I moved. Large items were still too heavy for me, but I remembered the power, the need when I made the Minions fly out of my way when I hungered for the Ja'pah who was hiding behind Espy's eyes, and I used that urgency to lift The Lady from the bed.

It worked, and I was so surprised that I dropped her. The guard, realizing time was running out, ran out of the room. I concentrated again, knowing my life was now in danger, and pulled The Lady through the air.

I ran after the guard, who was fiddling with something in his hand by a wall.

"Wait!" I commanded, and he froze.

When I reached him, I saw he wasn't moving. Steic! I froze him! I tried to release him, but my mind kept filling itself with fear that he was trying to leave me. I concentrated and he unfroze and began coughing as if he had been held underwater, unable to breathe.

The guards shouted in the next room.

"Go on!" I pointed to the device in the guard's hand, but he was still coughing.

Isdollem guards entered the living quarters, and I thought "protection" as they aimed and fired. A wall sprang up from my Qutcy, but some of the firing came through, hitting my partner in the leg.

He yelled in agony, ignoring his coughing fit, and immediately began hitting the device in his hand again. The wall rippled, and I jumped through, not waiting for the guard, pulling the floating Lady behind me.

And then I was falling.

I screamed as the sudden wind outside hit me and as I realized I had no footing. I wrapped my arms around The Lady in desperation, as if the limp body could save my life.

Float! The word shot in my head, and suddenly I stopped in the air. The rush of the power jolted through me, and then I stood suspended in air. I slowly allowed myself to breathe in the cold air, seeing the steam of my breath gently fall on the sleeping Lady that I still had in my grasp. Everything around me was silent as if also pausing to breathe, then suddenly, someone screamed above me. I watched the guard pop out of the wall and drop uncontrollably through the air. He flew past me in complete terror, kicking his legs while his arms flung wildly about him. Jerking myself out of my stunned state, I spread my fingers downward as if I were reaching for him and concentrated.

Float! I commanded twice, until he stopped in the air.

My fingers still pointing in his direction, I floated down to him, making sure I hadn't frozen him into not breathing. His eyes were still wild, but otherwise okay.

Shakily, the guard and I floated in the air, and I grabbed his face to take his attention from his fear. "Where do we go?"

He didn't answer as he looked down at the long fall below.

I pulled his hair. "Where?"

"Down, and under," he managed to say.

"Where down?"

He only pointed, and that's all I could get from him for the moment. I began to make an accelerated descent towards the ground as I heard the distant whirring of galers coming in our direction. Wherever we had to go, we had to make it there fast.

"Stop!" The guard shouted.

I thought he was only afraid, and I kept going.

"No, Stop! You passed it!"

I stopped and looked around. I didn't see anything.

"Up there," he pointed. I didn't understand. I floated back up anyway.

"Here," he said, reaching for the wall. There was a small brick slightly out of place.

The guard took out the device again, and the wall rippled. I floated us through it and found us back in the filthy tunnels Espy and I had climbed out of just minutes before. The guard began limping away and I followed, still pulling The Lady in the air.

We floated down the ladders, which I thought would make our escape swift, and we ran down the tunnels. Soon, tired, and our adrenaline spent, we began walking, and I knew this part of the journey would take hours, as it had before.

But no one was pursuing us, which was odd. And why was the escape route the same as the entryway? It didn't make sense, and we should have been overrun with guards by now. But I didn't have time to second-guess a cate already in the works.

I easily kept up with the guard, who limped ahead, and I wondered how much pain he was in or if he was losing blood. In any case, it wasn't stopping him from escaping down the tunnels.

Soon, I began to think we were lost. I expressed my concern to the guard, but he insisted that we were going the correct way. We traveled for more hours before stopping and resting. I fell asleep as soon as I lay down.

A young Wendh male climbed up a dirt wall in terror. Fire and smoke sprayed out down below from an exploding ship as he scrambled up the crater's edge. Something large moved below him, something evil. A large claw sprang at the child's ankle and missed. The Wendh screamed, flinging out six tentacles to hurry away from danger. A violent roar escaped the throat of the beast below as the child reached the edge of the crater and pulled himself to flat ground.

He wasn't safe yet, as the pursuing creature leapt up from the crater's wall and blocked the child's route of escape. It stood on six legs with an upright torso and two arms ending with pinchers instead of hands. Antennae waved up in the air from its smooth, bald head as two huge mandibles stretched out in preparation to close around the child's neck. Beady black eyes glared down at the Wendh with triumph as it charged towards the horrified child.

The Wendh jumped out of the way, using his speed and endurance to barely escape the beast's jaws. The giant collapsed, missing its intended target, and the child ran with blind terror, taking advantage of the moments that the stunned creature allowed as it gathered itself up from its fall.

The youngster could not outrun his pursuer; he was much too young and inexperienced, and his short legs could not gather much speed like an adult Wendh's would have. The beast was soon upon him, slamming down on the ground with a great rumble, causing the child to lose his footing. He fell and scrambled on to his back to see the beast come down upon him with its mandibles open.

A cry came from behind the stalker's prey, followed by a large blast of concentrated fire. The creature was hit right in its center, and in moments the fire spread to its body. As it screamed in agony, the child crawled back up to his feet and ran towards his rescuer.

Another weapon fire flew through the air, aimed right at the creature's torso, consuming it entirely. The beast ran around, wailing with high-pitched screams, and more fire shot in the air to add to the beast's torment. It fell down to the ground with a great thud as the smell of its death rose in the air.

The young Wendh reached his rescuer and stared at him with surprise. The male was not much older than himself, with large ears hanging down to his waist and small round eyes, which before they blinked, first appeared to be nonexistent.

"Welcome to Quuto," the strange Being smiled with a slit mouth.

# # #

I awoke slowly from the extraordinary dream, trying to comprehend why my mind would conjure up such a story. Perhaps because I felt pursued; perhaps because The Lady of Isdol slept near me, and her presence reminded me of execution and death.

I shrugged the strange dream away, telling myself that real danger existed now and we had to keep moving. Looking at the guard still sound asleep made me wonder how long we had slept. Hours, perhaps? Were we late for our rendezvous? I urged the guard awake, and he glanced at his qCarpus and commanded it for a time. It was early afternoon. He jumped up with complete surprise and we continued our journey with urgent determination.

I looked at The Lady, hoping she would remain asleep. Keeping her afloat wasn't hard. I felt a part of my mind constantly working, but not so troubling to me that I couldn't complain to myself about the walking. The sleep had made me stiff.

We finally came to another branch of the tunnel and saw something red and large on the ground. I stood to the side as the guard nudged it with his foot and it moved.

I heard a woman scream in terror before jumping to her feet. I immediately recognized the red cloth folded around the figure's body and the red hair, tangled and wild.

"You scared me!" The dancer hissed at the guard and then looked at me and the floating Lady.

The guard reached for his weapon. "Who are you?"

The female shrugged at the armed male and turned her attention to me. "Some mess you got yourself into! You know how long it took me to find where you were? I finally heard about this 'new Minion,' and then saw on the holoscreen that you were at Isdol, so I came here to find you. Did you know what I had to do to join up with this silly dancing group? They're not talented in the least! Then I had to watch you kidnap The Lady! Haven't you learned anything yet?"

I was too shocked by her bantering to figure out how she knew me. But then I stared at her red hair, and her bright green eyes flashed with a quick wink.

"Tokie?" I motioned to the guard to lower his weapon.

"Who else would it be?" she snapped.

I couldn't believe it! "What are you doing here? How--"

She interrupted me, "I've already told you. By The Name! If your mother only knew what you were doing . . ." she ran out of words.

The guard impatiently began to walk away down the left tunnel. "We don't have time for this! We're behind schedule as it is, and The Lady will be waking up any moment now."

"That's the wrong way!" Tokie yelled after him. "You're party is waiting for you this way. They've been waiting for an entire day."

The guard turned around and looked at me. I was just as shocked at this new twist as he was. But then I noticed that he seemed to be looking at me as if to say, 'Can I trust her?'

"It's alright," I said, grabbing a firm grip around The Lady's ankle. "Let's go this way."

I led the way with Tokie right behind me.

"Tokie, you should have gone home," I hissed without turning around. "It isn't safe here."

"I can take care of myself," Tokie abruptly answered, a statement I'd heard from her a lot lately; a statement that I probably should believe.

"We should not talk," the guard grunted behind us, trying to keep up with his injured leg. "We don't know who's listening."

"No one's listening," Tokie brashly said. "Why do you Beings get so paranoid in these kinds of situations? It's simply beyond me. You either do it or you don't, and deal with the consequences of your actions, whatever decision you make. Just accept--"

"Silence, Tokie!" My brief excitement at seeing her was over. Finishing this cate with her trailing behind would jeopardize our mission, but there wasn't anything I could do about it right now. "Just be silent. Can you do that for once? Be silent until we get where we need to be."

Tokie didn't answer, which actually surprised me. I turned to look at her, but she seemed to be interested in the tunnel surrounding us.

I wondered how she got down here and then figured she must had been on to me somehow. I didn't have a barrette this time, but then again, how did she know where we were meeting?

We had only walked perhaps an hour more before someone swung in front of me at a corner turn and barred my way.

It was a short Isdollem male wearing clean white pants and a shirt. It wasn't a guard; he didn't have the right attire.

"You're late," he said, glancing at The Lady and the three of us. "I was expecting two males and a female."

"Change of plans," I said suddenly. "The dancer is with me."

The Isdollem male didn't like it, and I didn't blame him. A change of plan in a cate was never a good sign. He motioned us to follow him anyway, and we walked through a wall into a spacious room filled with crates, equipment and a table lining one wall.

Four Beings were in the room. Two more Isdollem males stood near the crates, and I immediately recognized the green-robed Being, but standing next to him was someone roped in white; my white!

I went to Espy with a questioning look, but he signaled the one robed in my white, and she took off the robe and handed it to me. The female wasn't someone I recognized, but she was definitely dressed like a high-caste bawd.

"You're hours late," Espy reprimanded the guard. "What happened?"

While I put on the robe, the guard answered, "My partner had second thoughts and almost jeopardized the cate. He stalled me as he tried to figure out a way to tell The Lady of our plans and save himself. By the time I discovered what he was doing, I didn't have time to react but to kill him in front of her and release the gas. Our first four escape routes were blocked because of his betrayal. The fader never completed his part of the cate."

Espy quickly turned and looked at me. *Are you alright?* he mentally asked in his soothing voice.

Yes, I answered, knowing that he probably just figured out that I had to float in this cursed cate because of the botched plan. Brusquely I added, *I suppose you're going to tell me that this wasn't supposed to happen this way. This makes number two, Espy.*

He didn't reply, and I wondered what the Ja'pah would do to him. I finally asked, *Why didn't anyone follow us to the sewers?*

We had diversions, and duplicates of you, Espy answered, and then commanded out loud, "The Lady," indicating the royal female still floating in the air.

The short male went to her and pulled her to a table. I released my mental hold on her as the male went to work, placing tubes down her nose and mouth and covering her with brown mush. We all watched him work as he plugged the ends of the tubes to two large containers and continued covering The Lady in mush. When she was completely submerged, he surrounded her in white, shining sheets of highly thin metal.

The short Isdollem's style of concealing The Lady was quite something to see, and it reminded me of . . ..

Tokie was standing entirely too close to the working male, smiling and openly flirting with him. I glanced at Espy, who was busy talking to the prostitute and explaining our next step. I tried getting Tokie's attention, but she was too busy getting the attention of the short male, who smiled back at her.

I finally walked over to her. "How did you find me?"

Tokie backed away from the Isdollem so she could whisper, "I told you. The holoscreen. New Minion? Obvious? Remember?"

"Where were you this past cycle?"

Tokie let out an annoying breath. "Looking for you. Didn't you hear anything I said back in the tunnels?"

Actually, I wasn't paying much attention, but I asked her to repeat the story anyway.

"I lost you on Quuto. Those Minions have some technology that covers their tracks or something. See, look at that?" She pointed to the Isdollem working on the female and smiled at him again.

I took a step in front of her, blocking her view of the short male. "Clarify."

Tokie feigned a frown and began again. "Back in the alley, when we got jumped by those thugs, I turned into something when the Minions showed up. When I saw they had you, I tried to follow, but they had some kind of force field up, and the form I took couldn't penetrate it. By the time I changed shape, you and your new friends were gone. Those detestable Minions didn't show their faces for months. I had to go back home to tell your mother what happened, and to promise I wouldn't stop searching for you for the rest of your life." She emphasized "your"; still hinting that she would be around for quite some time after I and others succeeding me.

"But anyway," she continued, "I watched the holoscreen and tried to track down one of those Minions to see if he would lead me back to you. That wasn't much luck. As soon as I found one, he'd disappear. They never stay in one place for too long. It was just luck that you appeared on Isdol's holoscreen at one of The Lady's parties. Plus all of the talk of the new Minion--"

I regretted ever asking her to tell me the entire story. "I've heard enough." I glanced back over to Espy, and when I turned back to Tokie, she was standing next to the short Isdollem again. I stormed my way over to her. "I think you should let him work."

"She's not bothering me," the male said, his eyes remaining on Tokie.

"We need you to concentrate," I insisted.

"A job well done, is a job done repeatedly," he answered, and I gulped down my surprise as I recognized the Reuss saying.

"He looks like he knows exactly how to use his hands," Tokie candidly flirted.

"Come away." Espy had appeared silently by my side.

Tokie's smile faded as Espy handed her a medical device and indicated the guard. She obediently went to the guard and tended his wound.

Who is she? Espy mentally asked me.

Tokie. You remember her. My traveling companion. She's from my home world.

How did she get here?

She followed me. For her, the new Minion persona was quite betraying.

Espy had more questions, I knew, but didn't ask them. He instead turned around and went back to talk to the bawd, and when Tokie was finished healing the guard, he included her in the conversation. Espy had to do something with Tokie now that she was here.

I turned my attention back to the short Isdollem male: his mannerism, his movements, that Reuss saying. I slowly realized that this Reuss was Vrang. There wouldn't be that many other Reusses with the experience, and insanity, to take on a cate like this. It had to be him. And the other two? Who were they? The intoxicated Joya, perhaps? Superstitious Tagg, maybe, with his medallion hidden beneath his clothes? Why hire the Reuss again to kidnap The Lady? But then I answered my own question. They had succeeded once before, so why not? I would ask Espy later.

While Vrang worked, the other two Isdollem males took items out of the crates and carefully pieced them together to form the top and bottom half of a statue of one of Isdol's ancient gods no longer worshipped. It looked like several of the items we had already shipped from Isdol.

When the short male finished, all three picked The Lady up from the table and placed her in the statue, and expertly sealed it closed. The entire thing looked like an Isdol masterpiece.

Vrang looked it over, making sure every crack and crease looked authentic before saying, "Done. The green stuff will freeze her in about ten minutes and will stay that way indefinitely, but to unfreeze her in a healthy state, my recommendation would be less than ninety days. However, the oxygen tanks will only last sixty-one days."

"More than enough time," Espy stated confidently, and then mentally said to me, *It's time to go.*

The Isdollem males and the guard stayed behind with The Lady, possibly to take her where the other supplies were stored that were to be shipped off Isdol. The rest of us made our way out of the underground sewage tunnels.

# # #

We walked until we were among sentient Beings again and entered a small parking terminal. A four-seat galer was waiting for us. Tokie and the bawd climbed into the back while Espy and I rode in the front. We flew up to the rim of unlawful ground and were stopped behind a long line of other ships waiting for clearance to exit.

Patrols were everywhere, searching everything and everyone, shining their bright lights, making it appear like dawn in the underground world. It took hours to get through the line.

"Departing from and destination?" an Enforcer asked from his ship as a wave of light swept over us, making anything solid appear to be transparent. The light searched through the galer and into our very bones and skin.

"We're coming from Juleq's," Tokie leaned forward, no longer the redheaded dancer who greeted us in the tunnel. She was beautifully green-skinned, with dark green hair, pretending to be a bawd cosmetically covered to play a seductive role for her client.

"Perhaps you've heard of us?" Tokie leaned forward and placed a jeweled map on the back of the Enforcer's hand. "Come by some time."

"Not likely," the Enforcer grunted with distaste, but he didn't remove the jewel from his hand. He turned his attention to Espy. "I didn't know the famous Ja'pah Minions were into such things."

"We're into a lot of things, as you know, Enforcer," Espy respectfully said.

"And you'll be caught one day, too. Not everyone can evade the law forever." The Enforcer's eyes looked hungry for fame for catching such unlawful Beings, but he had nothing to charge us with but indulging in perverse sex, and that was legal. He waved us through.

When we reached our hotel, I was glad to be free from the tension of being on a cate, and I felt utterly exhausted. I assumed it was the floating and the lack of good rest.

Floating. Once I got my strength up, I thought I would float around the room and perfect this new ability, but only after a long rest. Only Wendhs with the mental ability of green or higher could actually float themselves. . . . wait. Was the Ja'pah green like my family? His power was very strong. Perhaps he was blue, but the blue range began the high-caste, and the Ja'pah, well, he was the Ja'pah. But then again, he wasn't exactly a true Wendh, either. He was something entirely different. A Wendh, yet not a Wendh.

Nonetheless, I had the power like my father's family before me, and I was going to use it every chance I got!

I headed for the shower while Espy and the bawd went out for dinner, continuing to portray a couple out for the night. Washing was a slight chore. Because I had to maintain my Minion identity, which meant I had to keep my cape on at all times, I couldn't feel the full effect of the warm, cleansing water. At least the cape didn't retain bacteria and it dried quite nicely, so I was still able to leave the bathroom feeling clean.

Tokie was waiting for me on the bed, the exact place where I had intended to indulge in a restful sleep. She had shed the green bawd physiology.

I held up my hand before she could speak. "I already heard your lecture, Tokie, and I don't intend to hear more of it. I just want to sleep, and you *will* allow me to sleep, understand?"

"I just have one question," Tokie said as I lay down.

"No questions," I turned my head away from her, inhaling deeply and exhaling as I relaxed from the tension of the past several days.

"Just one," Tokie bugged, "I--"

"No!"

"Please, Jetticia."

Her voice had changed, making me look at her. Her eyes were shining brightly, and she no longer had that annoying grin on her face. "The short male. You looked like you knew him."

"How do you know how I looked?" I snapped. "I had my hood on. No one could possibly see--"

"The male," Tokie pleaded. "What is his name, and where is he homed?"

I stared at her. "Why are you so desperate?"

"His name," Tokie didn't give up easily.

I sat up slightly, thinking back on how she had flirted with the short Isdollem male. I smiled. "You act like you're in heat or something. What's wrong with you?"

Tokie blinked, her long eyelashes waving as she turned her head. "He just seemed . . . familiar."

Before I could ask another question, the hotel host computer announced that a guest was inquiring for entry. I jumped up from the bed and looked at Tokie, who only shrugged. I had to make a decision to answer or to turn the unknown party away. Curiosity won that battle. Espy would want to know who had decided to knock on the door of a Minion's hotel room.

I asked the computer to display the image of the Being waiting in front of the door, and my mouth dropped, while Tokie beamed, at the image that was shown.

Immediately, I went to the living room, stood at the door and invited the short Isdollem male in.

"What happened? Did something go wrong?" I demanded.

He completely ignored me and went straight for Tokie, who stood in the middle of the room. After a few steps, he began to shimmer, and a red-haired male child, similar to a Human if it weren't for the pointed ears, stood in the place where the adult Isdollem once had. He wore perfectly fitted shorts, a green cap, and matching green shirt with large white collars. Long, white socks came up to his knees and shiny black-buckled shoes covered his small feet.

"Trang," he bowed in front of Tokie, his green eyes sparkling. "And aren't you a pretty sight."

"Tokie," she curtsied and giggled her delight. "I haven't come across another--" she glanced at me and changed her words, "one of my kind since . . . well for, like forever."

"So when shall we get started?" Trang grabbed her close and planted a long, sloppy kiss on her mouth. Pulling back, he said, "I know a great planet some distance from here--"

"No," Tokie frowned, "*I* know a place."

Trang continued to smile. "My place is better, I assure you."

Tokie tried to step back, but Trang wouldn't release her from his arms.

"It is custom for the female to choose," Tokie tried to remain polite. "Well, for some species anyway. Besides, you're not the one who will have an orgasm for an entire year."

I stared at the both of them, my mouth gaping. What in The Name was going on?

Trang kissed Tokie quickly on the lips. "As I am much, much older and wiser than you, I do know what's best for us."

Tokie shoved him back, causing him to fall on the floor. "Age has nothing to do with wisdom!" She shouted down at him. "I have seen stories, and possibly THE story, that would make you shimmer in envy."

"You don't know what stories I've seen!" The male child pouted on the floor, not bothering to get back up. "And I've probably seen a lot more stories than you have!"

"Silence, both of you!" I shouted, regaining my composure. "What is going on?"

"He started it!" Tokie pointed an accusing finger at Trang.

"No, you started!" Trang shot back.

"You started it!"

"No, you started!"

"You started it!"

Their bickering was starting to get to me. I covered my eyes. "Shut up!" *Oh please, Suphyz, don't let me have to deal with two of these annoying little pests.* I sat down on the couch to remedy this strange argument.

The two children stared at me and said in agitated unison, "You're interrupting our marriage proposal!"

My eyebrows rose. "Your what?"

They both ignored me and continued to bicker on where they should have their liaison and who had the better stories.

I went to bed, suppressing my urge to float them both right into a wall. Besides, they could talk more openly without my being there, and I didn't have to hear any more of their squeaky voices. They could keep their little secrets, too, because I wasn't a bit interested. I was only interested in getting some sleep. Hopefully, they could keep each other company long enough so not to interrupt my sleep. Maybe Tokie would go away with her betrothed, which would solve a lot of potential problems if she were to stay.

# # #

When I awoke, it was still night, and I found Tokie sleeping soundlessly next to me. I had thought she would be gone.

"We decided to go to both planets after this story," Tokie said with her eyes still closed, obviously awakening when she sensed I was conscious. "Part-time to my planet and part-time to his. It should be a wonderful mating experience." She yawned before adding, "That was Vrang, by the way. He said you were addicted to his sex, and that he was quite cruel to you sometimes. But you must forgive him, and be assured that your past relationship with him doesn't disturb me." With another yawn she added, "Now, please don't interrupt me while I sleep. I'm quite tired." With that, she turned over and began to snore.

I got up and found sleeping arrangements elsewhere. Her annoying attitude and sudden surprises were really testing me to the limit.

# # #

Espy and the bawd came in that morning and slept until the afternoon. The bawd, who I later found out was the owner of Juleq's and was indeed Juleq herself, stayed with us a few more nights. All four of us, with Tokie again in bawd attire, went out to eat and attended shows like normal Beings. News of The Lady's second kidnapping was the only thing on the vids and holoscreens, and I turned them off. It made me antsy; why were we were still on this planet?

Five nights later we headed back to the unlawful grounds, waited in line for another hour for entrance, and dropped off Tokie and Juleq at Juleq's. Tokie, of course, pretended to walk into the building, but came back out in some invisible form or air particle. I didn't see how she got back into the galer. She just appeared again when we were back at our hotel. When I asked her how she did it, she only shrugged and went on some tangent on the sights she wanted to see while she was on Isdol and her excitement of mating with Trang, which she mentioned almost every hour. Espy told her she was not to be seen anywhere with us and that she had to go see the sights by herself. She pouted, of course, saying it wouldn't be as much fun, but contended because she had no other choice.

Espy and I continued to barter with merchants and send crates offworld, which was six times harder than it had been when we first arrived. Every large crate that was inspected made my heart stop, hoping she was camouflaged correctly, seeing that the lights penetrated through every solid object. But whatever Vrang, uh, Trang, used must have reflected the rays. I never found out which day The Lady was actually shipped out.

We stayed on Isdol for another three weeks among angry Isdollems who demanded retribution. It was tense on the planet, and being a Minion didn't help. No one ever accused us; instead, they seemed to turn all of the blame toward their rival planet, Jancso. Only *they* would have had the gall to kidnap The Lady a second time, and from The Lady's home planet at that! No one seemed to notice the ascendance of The Lady's brother and cousin as they slowly and eagerly took control of the throne in "the name of The Lady." Not even the voting council appeared to be aware of it.

I was more than happy when we departed from Isdol; so glad, in fact, that I didn't bother with questions of our next destination.

We left "the Pure Planet" to jump to Deluxar to trade the items we acquired from Isdol. Deluxar was always a good place to go to sell exotic items. Then, we traveled to three more planets, selling our items, playing out our part, as if someone were watching us. One could never be too careful.

Tokie obediently stayed out of sight, running her own errands at every stop we made. I began to believe her obedience most have come from her mind-clutter about Trang--either that, or Espy's firm hand. Either way, everything went smoothly during the two additional weeks it took to complete our bartering. Two weeks too long. I was beginning to feel my hunger.

Chapter 14   Clarifications

"Hungry, aren't you?" Tokie leaned over me as I sprawled out on the bed. "I think we're flying back to your new home now."

"How do you know?" I inquired. "Espy never tells us where we're going." Shuddering from another shot of pain, I tried not to concentrate on the hunger and think of something else. Tokie's presence, at the moment, would be quite distracting.

I turned to look at her, gritting my teeth. "How do you know so much about . . . things?"

Tokie shrugged like she usually did when queries were about her identity.

"I'm serious," I pried. "How do you know?"

"If you have a long lifespan, things just seem to make sense a lot more quickly." She jumped away from me and began to dance in the middle of the room to an unheard melody.

"So what story are you and Trang seeking?"

Tokie continued to dance. "No one in particular."

"I heard you. You said THE story."

She shrugged again and changed the subject. "He is quite spectacular, you know. I can't wait!"

I suspected the "he" she was referring to was Vrang from her wishful type of look when she spoke. A part of me wanted to let her suffer under his hands, but my conscience took the better of me. This wasn't sitting well with me.

"Tokie," I said, my serious tone getting her attention. "Vrang-
-"

"Trang," she corrected.

"Trang," I said under my breath, "he isn't a very good male. He's--"

"I told you, you have to forgive him." She stopped dancing. "He just got caught up with the way things are here. It happens sometimes, even to me, three millenniums ago, or was it four?" And before I could interject, she continued. "And don't tell me I'm in that silly 'It won't happen to me' mindset, because it *won't* happen to me. He's back on track now, because I'm with him, and that's all that matters . . . and the story, of course."

I didn't argue with her. She was always right about things, especially when she got so demanding. "About that story you both were talking about--"

"We're here," she said suddenly and danced out of the room.

I grimaced and rolled my eyes. Why did I even bother? I should just stop talking to the little imp, period. I rolled over on my side and forced myself up from the bed, wavered a moment, and then stood up.

Espy greeted me at the door and helped me out of the ship. We entered a hangar, and its familiarity gave me a sort of calming effect, like when I returned to my home world. We were back at the Ja'pah's crypt.

Tokie skipped ahead of us and then circled around and skipped behind us, as she didn't know where to go. We took the grand hall down to the dining area, where Voice and Reso stood with their backs to us and their hoods down. When we came nearer, I saw that they faced the Ja'pah, who sat in a large chair that did not match the other chairs that were normally here. The table and chairs were gone. The setup reminded me of a small throne room, like on Ytieria.

Voice turned towards Tokie, his eyes dark and shining. "What have we here?" The Ja'pah spoke through him.

Tokie curtsied her greetings with a large grin, but in the next beat, she stomped her foot, causing a sharp crackle to echo in the room, and pointed a finger at the Ja'pah with a scowl spread across her face, her green eyes flashing.

"How dare you!" she shouted, jolting me out of my weakened state. "How dare you put her in this position!"

I knew that Tokie was a bit off sometimes, but this was too unconventional even for her. I was too shocked to stop her.

"You should know better than that! You should know better than this!" She swung her pointed finger in my direction and then returned it to the Ja'pah. "How dare you allow the pattern to run like this?"

Voice took a step towards Tokie, and so did Espy.

"Interesting," Espy said as he witnessed Tokie's brilliant, shining eyes for the first time. Pulling back his green hood, he investigated her more closely with his large eyes. "I have never seen the like. She's perfectly formed in every way. I see no power in her . . . yet . . . something--"

"What is it that you want, little one?" Voice spoke again through the Ja'pah. "How can I be of service?"

Tokie walked towards the seated Ja'pah, but Espy barred her way.

"It's alright," Voice raised his hand simultaneously with the Ja'pah. "I sense no bad intent in her. In fact, I sense no evil at all."

Espy reluctantly stepped out of the way and allowed Tokie to come nearer.

"I want you to do what you must to protect this child." Tokie's voice had changed, and the elder, maternal tone bellowed through. "Do what you refuse to do, because time is running short. The Xarthrens are regrouping, as you know. They will not stop until they have won."

The Ja'pah entwined his fingers, not acknowledging what Tokie had just implied, but my eyes widened at the declaration. The Xarthrens were returning?

"It may be several more cycles, but that is not enough time to pull the Four Quadrants back together, the upper and lower worlds," Tokie glanced at Voice but continued to speak directly to the Ja'pah. "Everyone has become too lax, too arrogant, too divided. The Isdollems have become too greedy, and construction and new technology has almost come to a complete stop. Do what you were born to do, Ja'pah, and do it quickly. And in the meantime, do what you must to protect your mate!"

Silence filled the air and I looked around at the stunned Minions, who stared at Tokie and then back at the Ja'pah, anxiously waiting for an order to do something.

Tokie then smiled, her glowing eyes dimmed away, and she locked her hands behind her back and began twisting in playfulness. "Now, that's said and done," her childish voice returning, "what do you have to eat around here? I'm famished!"

There was a moment of silence while Tokie twisted back and forth in her innocent manner, before the Ja'pah himself spoke. "Leave me and take our new ally to the guest room and feed her."

Voice, no longer taken over by the Ja'pah, opened his mouth to protest, but closed it suddenly. Waving to his brothers, he did as instructed, and they turned to leave the room with Tokie skipping behind them.

I also turned, but was instantly held still by a force and a mental whisper, *Not you.*

I turned back around as everyone else rounded the corner, and faced the Ja'pah.

Come here, he commanded, leaning back in his chair.

I nervously glanced back to no one in particular and timidly made my way to him. When I was near, a tentacle wrapped itself around my waist, forcing me to take a seat on the Ja'pah's lap. His head tilted down to my neck, and I heard him inhale my scent.

His hand raised up and his fingers found my nipple, which he stroked from outside my cowl. That single gesture shot sparks through my veins.

"My Minions tell me that they had lost their connection with you for quite a few hours," his voice rumbled through me, and an uncomfortable feeling began to consume my insides. "Tell me, did you sleep in the waste tunnels of Isdol?"

I suddenly felt like a weapon was going to be raised and fired at close range through my stomach. Relaxing during a cate was a broken rule, but that cate had lasted for more than normal hours. Sleep was inevitable.

I gave a meek reply. "Yes."

His fingers left my nipples and caressed my neck. "Did you dream?" He inhaled more of my hungering scent, tilting my head slightly and then turning my face to his.

I stared into the darkness of his hood, remembering the Xarthren beast that pursued the Wendh child in my nightmare.

"Yes," I answered, unable to deny that it was just a weird dream. The Ja'pah was the child. The dream was of the past. The dream was another cord of our strengthening bond, which the Minions were preventing in order to hide the Ja'pah's identity from me.

He moved, making me jerk back instinctively, ready for a strike, but he lifted me up in his arms instead, carrying me out of the dining room. "Tell me about it," he said as we headed to the room with the fountain and the guarding beasts erected at their posts. " . . . Afterwards."

His room was silver and black, but no decorations covered its walls and few items occupied its space. There was the huge bed with bedposts, a bathing pool, a cabinet to the far right, and an empty desk and high-backed chair.

He carried me to the bed, laying me gently down on its soft curves, and wasted no time pulling off my cloak and bodysuit, before then slowing down. He took me as if he had all the time in the world; lingering here, than lingering there, slowly penetrating, gently kissing. It was intense gentleness, allowing me to moan my pleasure instead of screaming, allowing me to move and rock dreamily with him.

All the time in the world . . ..

The gentleness gradually increased to ravenous thrusting, sometime after the third joining. I had just enough voice left to scream my pleasure before his teeth sank into my neck, absorbing my blood before sending his own burning through my veins.

# # #

I woke up several days later in my own quarters, not noticing much of the metamorphosis that was going on within my body. But I did notice that no one was around. I searched the dining hall and knocked on the Minions' colorful doors, but received no answer. I finally asked Bymé where the Minions were on the meteoroid, and she directed me to the training room.

I immediately saw the change of the room when I walked through the door. The room was too small and dark. Reso, Espy and Tokie stood in the darkness, the only light coming from a window in the wall, which they all faced. Curiously, I approached, wondering what they were looking at. Voice was standing on the opposite side of the window in a white room in a size still too small, even if merged with the room in which I was standing, to be the room where I had trained. They must have created a room within a room, but why?

My eyes lay on the dark capsule next to Voice, and I recognized it as the black casing that Reso and I had picked up from Jancso. Opposite Voice lay The Lady of Isdol, bound to a white block.

She was awake, her eyes filled with murderous intentions as she stared at Voice, who tapped lightly on the capsule's controls.

"What's going on?" I asked.

Tokie hushed me. "You're about to witness a change in the story."

Suddenly, The Lady shouted, "You'll be given a thousand deaths, Minion, for kidnapping The Lady of Isdol! I will personally see you tortured until the last breath escapes my body!"

Before she could bluster on, Voice calmly interrupted, "Just one moment more, my Lady." He tapped a few more buttons, watched the screen, and stepped back. "There."

Nothing happened. I turned to question Espy, but then the capsule opened and Vortsi stood inside, his eyes still closed. He was a magnificent Wendh, a pure reflection of his royal blood. His stance was full of confidence and his movements rippled of power. Even The Lady gaped at him as he slowly opened his eyes and took a step forward.

"What . . ." The Lady stammered, "What is the meaning of this?"

"My Lady," Voice introduced, "Vortsi, the royal cousin of Imperial TeNeil."

"I . . . I don't understand."

I didn't either, as I watched Voice bow his leave.

"Don't leave me!" The Lady commanded, pulling on her restraints. "I command you! Release me!"

"I am sorry that I cannot comply," Voice intoned. "I must take my leave."

"No!" The Lady almost shouted with entreatment. "Do not leave me with that . . . that thing!"

"Do not be worried," Voice spoke to Vortsi, whose eyes never left The Lady. "Her suicide chip was removed before we revived her. Simply call me if you need anything." Voice bowed again.

"I will not need anything," Vortsi finally spoke, never moving his gaze from The Lady.

Voice left through the door and suddenly appeared in our part of the room. I opened my mouth to question him, but he waved his hand to quiet me and pointed to the scene before us.

Vortsi took several steps towards The Lady, whose restraints undid themselves. The Lady leaped from the white block and ran towards the door Voice had exited. It was a flimsy move. She was caught by Vortsi's tentacles before she could even touch the door. Screaming, The Lady tried using her fists and nails on the Wendh, but he calmly carried her back to the block, and there, he tore at her clothes.

I stood stunned as the royal cousin stripped The Lady naked underneath him and forced his erection inside her. The Lady's scream pierced my ears as well as my heart, and I turned away. The Minions and Tokie watched as if they were in front of a holoscreen, unaffected by the scene that played out in front of them. But her screams that had pierced the air were quickly replaced by her moans. I turned around to see her clinging to Vortsi's back, forcing him to dive into her again and again. Then the window darkened and a light went on where the five of us stood.

"See?" Voice smiled, "doesn't take long at all." He laughed. "Those ancient historical archives were quite accurate about Wendhs and Isdollems mating." He laughed again. "That was fast."

I was slightly shocked as well. It *was* fast. I have seen the struggle of Humans taken by Wendhs on my home planet, and how they tried to resist a Wendh's touch. It took a bit of time. And Voice found that the Isdollems were not completely untouched by Wendhs. There was a time when Wendhs did have them as mates. I wondered briefly where that information was securely hidden. I wondered if my own mother was truly the first Human that a Wendh had had The Calling for. I shook my head. It seemed that as long as there had been Wendhs and space travel, every species has been touched.

Espy took Tokie by the hand and, before walking out, said to Voice, "We still need a month to make sure the union is complete."

"Nonsense," Voice walked out into the hanger, "Isdollems join faster with Wendhs than any species in the universe. Three days at the most."

I ran in front of Voice. "What's going on? And why am I the last one to know about this?"

"She always gets like this," Tokie interposed.

I cut my eyes at her and blocked Voice's way.

He gave up. "Vortsi is mating with The Lady."

"I saw that!" I spat. "What does it mean?"

"It means," Tokie mocked, "that Isdol can't be greedy with their precious reoet crystals and we can all get on with building better ships, constructing more star gates, and find a wormhole to the Xarthren's home world so we can crush them before they can completely regroup and come back here and destroy the Four Quadrants. That's what it means."

I hated her.

I wanted to rudely remark, "Why would the Ja'pah care about another Xarthren invasion?" but the thought of the dream held my tongue instead.

Fortunately, Espy pulled Tokie away and headed back to the grand hall with Reso following, saying, "We're going to eat. There's something I would like you to try."

Tokie beamed.

Thank you, I mentally spoke to Espy, and he smiled his reply. "Now," I said again to Voice, "can you start from the beginning?"

Voice shrugged. "It's just like your friend said. We need the reoet crystals, and the Isdollems are quite stingy about them, as you know. The Underworld knows the nature of the Xarthrens, and the high-caste refuses to acknowledge it. The Xarthrens are reorganizing and will come back. We need to be prepared. Vortsi and The Lady's union will make this possible." Voice walked around me and mentally broadcasted his hunger and his wish to join the others for dinner.

Dinner? It was dinnertime? But, no, wait. I couldn't let his simple answer appease me. "Vortsi had a Calling for The Lady? How did you know?"

"The Ja'pah knew," Voice simply answered, which said enough. The Ja'pah seemed to know just about everything. "We just took the opportunity to help Vortsi along. Without our help, he would have been killed before he set foot on Isdol. Reso was right. We had to go in his place and retrieve The Lady for him. It was much too risky for him to attempt it on his own. His hunger would have overwhelmed all other senses."

"And their union will allow Wendhs to control the reoet crystals," I walked behind Voice with full understanding. "Specifically the royal family."

"Exactly. Isdollems easily succumb to a Wendh's touch, as you just witnessed. They can't hold hatred in their hearts for one or two cycles like other species can. Therefore, they're afraid of being completely controlled by Wendhs. Thus, they are implanted with suicide chips hidden somewhere in their bodies in case a Wendh in Calling captures them. It is understandable, but it is also inevitable that they will someday be overrun by Wendhs and be forced to relinquish their fear and hatred and trust that the Wendhs will only do well by them."

"How were you able to remove the chip?" I questioned. "Trying to remove it means certain death for the host."

Voice smiled. "We retrieved the codes from Deluxar," and with that, we entered the dining room.

The table and chairs had returned to their place, with an extra chair for Tokie. A spred of food covered the table's surface, and Tokie's mouth was already stuffed. I sat down to eat with the others, now realizing how starved I was, having spent the past few days asleep.

But I still had questions. "Why did you let her go the first time? The Reuss had her just where you wanted her." I gathered the food on my plate and looked up at Voice for more answers.

Reso retorted to his whispered voice, "That wasn't us," and Voice concluded, "We suspect it was Yolikeg who had her kidnapped the first time."

"The Lady's cousin?" That didn't make sense. "Why not her brother, Torshincal? He's the next in line, and Yolikeg is probably the six or seventh royal in line."

"Torshincal? Much too weak," Espy replied. "Plus, he loves his sister too much, but he's also a puppet for Yolikeg. He practically does whatever his cousin says."

"Didn't you see how quickly they took over The Lady's throne?" Tokie smacked on her food. "Yolikeg is so stuck beside The Lady's brother that you would probably need more than a laser to cut them away from each other. It's quite obvious."

I ignored her. "You think Yolikeg knew about Vortsi?"

Voice frowned. "Yes, or at least knew of someone's intention to kidnap her. He didn't just want her kidnapped, he wanted her dead."

I looked at the Minions and knew they were dealing with a fader somewhere among their command. That was three times now that someone had botched their cate regarding Vortsi and The Lady.

"It's no longer important now," Voice said, chewing. "What is important is their union, and the preparation for attacking the Xarthrens."

"More, please," Tokie held out her empty plate, and for once I had to agree with her, and refilled mine as well.

I ate ten plates of food before mentally hearing the Ja'pah call me back to his room.

The Ja'pah didn't want to discuss my dream as I had thought, but attended to our other needs. The time apart since I had been away on the cate had been too long, and we both had to make up for lost time.

Chapter 15   Fader

Don't tire yourself, Reso whispered in my mind. *We have some unfinished business to attend to. Meet me in the hangar.*

I looked across the training room, losing my concentration and immediately was chided for it as an iron rod swooped down and struck me against my right shoulder.

"Steic! Reso!" I dodged another iron swinging down in front of me. "Couldn't you have picked a better time?"

Concentrate, Espy mentally reprimanded, knowing very well that Reso had thrown me off balance, but not blaming him.

Anger got me through the rest of the obstacle course, and when I was done, I threw the fleiking flower down at Espy's feet.

"You could try siding with me for once," I yelled at Espy.

Espy ignored my rude behavior, bent down and retrieved his prize. "I can't. It's the longevity of our friendship, Maheir Jetta."

As he took in the scent of the flower, I smiled as I stormed by him and headed for the hangar. He reminded me somewhat of my brother, which was shocking, as I didn't see much of a similarity about the two. Perhaps it was the feeling.

"Where are you going?" Tokie sprinted into the hangar, coming from nowhere, as usual. She must have gotten by Voice somehow, because Voice followed her into the hangar with an exasperated look on his face.

"I wanna go. Where are you going?" Tokie headed straight for Reso. How did she know so much?

"This will be a quick run," Espy stepped in. "They will return soon. Let me show you--"

"I want to go!" Tokie shimmered into Birken, the Trecian male. "Birken can help. Birken is strong."

"Birken," Voice interrupted, "will stay here as ordered. This cate is for Reso only."

"She go," Birken/Tokie pointed an accusing finger. "I can go, too!"

"Come, Tokie--" Espy began.

"Birken!" Tokie snapped.

"Birken," Espy corrected himself. "You can learn a more interesting story from Voice."

"Story . . . ?" Tokie was distracted, and Reso and I entered the ship and left before she could begin a tantrum.

"I didn't think we were ever going to get free," I sat down next to Reso and he pointed behind me.

"Wash and put on your cloak. We're going to go see some old friends of yours."

I didn't bother to ask who these friends might be as I made my way to the sonic cleaning area. I would find out soon enough.

# # #

Several hours and jumps later, I was back in my old life again, and feeling uncomfortable about it. Hentpki. Not only were we on my second home planet, but we were heading to The Mills itself, where my old life as a university student had ended and my new life as a thief had begun.

We entered The Mill in such a way that made me believe we weren't expected. Reso used a device similar to what Espy had used in the waste tunnels of Isdol, making the wall shimmer and flexible enough for us to walk through it. What he held in his hand was so high-tech that the Reuss would kill to have one.

We ended up high in the air, balancing on railings and looking down into the room where Tagg had shot at me.

Sadotch was there, sitting hugely in his floating chair and munching happily from the container in front of him. Vrang stood in front of him with several Reusses flanked by his side. He spoke to a Quattor, the second one I've ever seen, who could have been Karplus with his large four arms and single ponytail hanging down from a bald head, if he hadn't been the color of crimson instead of blue. The Quattor had nine of his companions next to him. One spoke to Tagg on the side.

I wondered why we were here, and then remembered the Reuss's involvement with The Lady's kidnapping. Payment was in order.

A voice rang out below, filled with animosity.

"The settlement was, eight, not six," Vrang's voice rasped. He held his short stature high, but he only came up to the Quattor's waistline. "The cate was clean, flawless. Why do you insult us with this payment?"

"It is not my fault that you forget the amount due," the Quattor voiced. "The payment was six, not eight."

"Perhaps," Tagg stepped forward, "we can come to some kind of agreement. We can take this portion now, and be given the rest later." Tagg fingered his talisman with the royal child, making it reflect off of the Quattor's torso.

"No," the Quattor scrunched his face into a frown. "This is what we settled upon."

Reso tilted his head and mentally hissed, *Something's wrong.*

"Hmmm?" I was so interested in what was going on below that I had to think back on what Reso had just said. "What?"

I hear something, he tilted his head to the opposite side. He hissed again in my mind, and I realized he was mimicking the sound that he heard.

"Come now, sentients," Sadotch swung his chair slightly, his rolls jiggling, and his small arms paused momentarily from stuffing food into his mouth. "I'm sure we can come to some—"

The hissing was apparent to me now, and I looked behind the Quattor to see his back rippling. Four of his partners had covertly moved back as everyone's eyes were on Vrang and the Quattor's growing argument. Then the Quattor's back exploded open, and black objects burst out, caught by the Quattar's four partners, who were simply standing and waiting. Electric fire sprang out from the weapons as soon as they were in the hands of the paying party. Several Reusses went down before they realized what was happening.

Whatever kind of weapons they had were undetected by the Reuss's alarms, and they only seemed to work once. After the first fire, the Beings began using the sharp edges of the weapon as knives to attack. They continued finishing off the Reuss that were still standing.

"Reso!" I bent forward, watching my past family being butchered. How could they not see that coming?

"We did not come for this, Jetta." Reso turned around. "We must go. Let this resolve in its own way."

"But—" I watched Vrang take down one of his attackers, and get struck by another. "We have to help."

"This is no concern of ours." Reso was walking away. "Besides, we have endangered you more than we should have. The Ja'pah—"

Tagg was pinned down by the large Quattor, taking blows to the chest by all four fists. Tagg's tentacles tried to grip the massive body and whip him across the face and chest, but they weren't strong enough to push the Quattor off. One of the

Quattor's hands snatched the medallion from Tagg's chest and sent it skittering across the floor. Tagg was losing.

I jumped down from the railing.

"Jetta!" Reso's once soft voice became a shriek of panic.

I landed softly on the ground right in front of a pursuing enemy whose arms were raised high in the air to give a fleeing Reuss a deathblow. Seeing a white-cloaked Minion stunned him, which gave me a chance to knock him off his feet and kick his head into unconsciousness. The Reuss I saved got up to her feet, too shocked to see another attacker behind her. Flipping over her head, I landed two feet on the assailant's chest, knocking him straight through the air and hitting one of his partners in the face.

I turned back to the direction of the Quattor, who continued to bash on Tagg, who was rapidly losing strength. I rushed over, dodging onslaughts of fists and knives, and reached the Quattor to snatch his black ponytail from his head. A howling roar filled the room as the Quattor grabbed the back of his head, his attention no longer on the Wendh that lay helpless beneath him. Turning his large mass around, he faced me with rage and eyes lusting for murder. And in those eyes, I saw a memory of *a Quattor dominating a Wendh youth and suddenly screaming in pain from black, rapid movements made by the Wendh's piercing speed.*

I didn't wait for Quattor to send his arms flying towards me as I went for the pressure points of his body, striking with quick jabs and punches at every part I innately knew. The pain of his ponytail along with the agony of my blows made him roar, and he stumbled and fell over himself. A passing attacker ran behind me, and I stooped down, sending out my leg, causing her to trip. She fell with such force on her head that she lay stunned long enough for me to snatch the weapon she carried from her hands.

The Quattor was on his knees and was beginning to regain his rage and strength. I had to keep him down. I took the weapon to his arm, slicing through it like a carving knife cutting through juicy fat. He didn't have time to scream before I sliced another arm, and another. He fell on his back when I took his last arm and dropped the weapon on his chest.

I looked around to see that the Reuss were now on the winning side and taking care of the rest of the faders. I turned my attention back to Tagg. He was gathering himself up, black blood oozing from several wounds in his chest. He was still stunned and weak, but he would heal. Finding his talisman on the floor, I took it to him.

"Maheir," Tagg politely said as I walked up to him. "Ja'pah Minion. I am in your debt."

The way he spoke to me with such respect and awe made me sanguine. I couldn't speak, and only gesture I could muster was a slow nod.

"Damn snipers!" Sadotch yelled, obviously unharmed. I suppose the attackers were going to save him for last. He was harmless when it came to fighting anyway. "Vrang, why didn't you see those . . . those things!" He pointed to one of the weapons lying directly in front of him.

Vrang limped over to Sadotch. "It was encased in the Quattor's flesh. How was I supposed to know?"

"Perhaps a fader is among us," a fellow Reuss suggested. "I'm sure Tagg's security should have detected something."

"No," Tagg left me and limped over to stand in front of Sadotch. Typical Wendh. He could be on his deathbed, but wouldn't allow a single person to know it. He took the weapon from the ground. "These are simple weapons. My equipment would not have detected it, but it will now."

"Take that," Sadotch pointed a small arm in the Quattor's direction, "and the rest away, and get our profit--what there is of it."

He turned his chair around and looked in my direction. As if his life had not just been in jeopardy, he asked, "Ah, Senses, new Ja'pah Minion. What did we do to be graced with your presence here?"

"Payment," Reso, who stood next to the walls, watching the action, stepped forward from the shadows. "The cate we had you do. We're here to pay you, and I assure you it will go much more smoothly than those who preceded us."

"Faders," Sadotch spat. "We've been too close to elimination too many time this cycle. That Jetta is behind this, I tell you. Our greatest cate yet, The Lady and the Hotel Quitimah, and then this."

My insides stung from the accusations. I had almost forgotten that they had branded me a betrayer.

"You must admit," Tagg came forward, "that taking The Lady from her home world was much more grand than taking her from a simple hotel. And more profitable."

This heightened the Reuss's mood, and they smiled and laughed. Bragging about great cates always lifted poor spirits.

"Speaking of The Lady," Reso interrupted, his low tones penetrating the laughter. "Since we did a service for you, perhaps you could do another one for us."

We? I almost had to laugh. He did nothing but watch.

"We did one already, Minion," Sadotch gulped. "Another will double the price."

That was why I began working with Sadotch. He was reasonable and knew when to pull out from a streak that may become too dangerous. The Reuss's eyes, on the other hand, began to glitter for another chance at a game.

"No, Sadotch, more business between you and I would be much too soon for the Ja'pah's tastes," Reso softly shrugged the offer away. "It is information that I require."

Sadotch quietly munched as he mulled over the offer. Looking around at wounded and dead faders brought him to a conclusion. "Ask, Minion."

Reso didn't hesitate. "The Lady's cate from the Hotel Quitimah--who hired you for that?"

Only Sadotch would have the answer for that, and the rest of the Reuss turned to look at him. They, too, thought that would be interesting information to know.

"Yolikeg," Sadotch frankly stated. Confidentiality was essential to the Reuss and all honorable thieves, but Sadotch gave up information as easily as singing a song if there was payment involved.

Reso bowed. "The Lady's cousin. Yes, we expected as much." Then turning his head slightly to me, he added, "And as you gave such information to us, allow me to return some. The fader who destroyed your first cate with The Lady at the Hotel Quitimah was the Ja'pah."

Stunned into silence, the Reuss turned to each other. I heard one whisper, "She did have the sign of Ja'pah . . .."

I looked at Vrang, who stood in silence. He knew I wasn't the fader. I was sure Tokie must have mentioned that to his Trang persona, yet he said nothing. It was just like him to not care about anyone but himself. I wondered, again, if Tokie really knew what she was getting into.

Reso bowed, dropped a single chip to the ground, and left the room. I followed behind him, but remembering that I had Tagg's medallion still in hand, I turned back around. I caught Tagg a bit off-guard when I approached him and presented him with the good luck charm with the royal child emblem that was so easily torn from his neck.

I stepped close to him, very close, and slightly tilted back my hood.

Tagg's lips parted in shock as his eyes saw the face of the half-breed who had taken down a Quattor in front of his very eyes. With a smile, this half-breed, this mongrel, this abomination, this Hybrid, who had saved this superior Wendh from a Quattor and put him in awe, gave him a smile and said, "No debt is needed."

When I stared at the lovely Tagg, I suddenly realized how unremarkable he actually was. He was only a petty thief, after all, something I had never realized a cycle ago. Why did I ever need acceptance from him? He had never expanded into more than what he was. Every Wendh had dreams and aspirations much higher than this. He should have been sitting in Sadotch's chair instead of playing this role for so many cycles. I was a green Wendh, a royal on my planet, and mate to the Ja'pah. He was probably no better than an orange, or probably a red. I must have been utterly blind to not realize this before, but the timing of this knowledge now was ever so much sweeter.

I walked away from the stunned Wendh, feeling taller and stronger.

Chapter 16   Imperial

A little over a week passed on the meteoroid before we all were on the move again, and surprisingly we went together. I was donned in an elegant white, shimmering gown with Tokie disguised as a diamond tiara on top of my head, but my cloak covered the spectacular attire. I knew it would be in view sometime during this next cate, but I didn't wear the utiq oil to disguise my features. Perhaps later I would be handed the oil.

Espy, Reso and Voice flew in their individual ships while for the first time, I flew with the Ja'pah. Vortsi and The Lady were put to sleep--a precaution to keep the route to the Ja'pah's crypt a secret--and were placed aboard Espy's ship. During the royal mates' stay, they probably thought they were in some building on a planet somewhere, but they would never know, as neither of them were let out of the training room. With their attention steely focused on one another, they didn't seem to mind.

I sat next to the Ja'pah and watched the rest of the ships that flanked us, and then shoot off in opposite directions. We stayed by the meteoroid some minutes more, with silence filling the ship. It made me nervous.

Your dream . . .. his voice rumbled through my thoughts.

By this time, I had wanted to forget about it. He hadn't brought the subject back up, and I was actually fine about not talking about it. Yet now, before a cate of all times, he asked me and waited for an answer. I looked out the window to concentrate on a star to steel my nerves.

"I saw," I hesitated and then turned to face him. He was my mate. I shouldn't have to fear or worry about retribution. I was his life as he was mine. Even Tokie had told him that and even she, with her annoying personae, had no fear. Did she know him?

"I saw," I repeated, "you being attacked by a Xarthren and . . . Espy saved you."

He didn't reply, but sat there in silence.

I continued on. "A ship crashed on Quunto, a Xarthren ship."

I was going to talk more about the weapon Espy used on the Xarthren and the fear that I felt from the Wendh child (or was he Wendh)? but he mentally started the ship, and we jumped from the meteoroid to the middle of nowhere and then to a star gate where several high-caste ships waited for entrance.

I could recognize the Imperial's star gate from anywhere. Though I had only seen it from holoscreens, its size and nature was indistinguishable. Giving off a golden tint, its round structure displayed the carved symbols of the houses that had reigned since the forming of the Four Quadrants--nine in all.

The ships that were lined up for entrance were just as magnificent, and I wondered if the Imperial was hosting one of his balls that he loved so much, some months after the Seven Day Fest. There were other ships waiting for entrance, but only to go to the neighboring planets next to the Imperial and the Wendhs' home world, Zendyllic. I assumed that's what we were also doing. The Ja'pah never went to the Imperial's home, whether he was invited or not, and the Imperial TeNeil did not want to find himself amid that kind of company, anyway, being that the Ja'pah was, yet was not, his equal.

Our ship was scanned for possible illegal or harmful substances, and we were allowed entrance through the gate. The jump was fast, and soon we were in the galaxy where Wendhs were first created. Even the stars looked high-caste and luxurious.

I sat on the edge of my seat as we soared through space and headed to--

I stared at the Ja'pah and back at the Wendhs' home world. Then panic shot through me. *What are we doing here?*

Shhh, the Ja'pah quieted me, and I sucked in my breath from embarrassment. I didn't know that I had mentally broadcasted my fear, but the shock of landing on the home world was overwhelming.

Perhaps we were escorting Vortsi back home. He had been very thankful for our help in gaining his mate, an Isdollem at that! Would we be given some kind of an award? Perhaps that was it.

The Ja'pah guided us smoothly into the Imperial's hangar after being scanned yet again by security. Vortsi must have provided specific codes to enable us to land here; otherwise, we would have been turned to fiery crisps. Perhaps his rescue would be announced when we arrived.

I watched the high-caste exit their vehicles and walk elegantly with their premium attire to the palace's grand entrance. We, on the other hand, stayed aboard the ship . . . for several hours.

It was restless waiting. I had never been so anxious in my life. Uneasy thoughts flew in and out of my head, hoping that we were on an actual invite and that this was not some kind of cate that would get us all killed. This was the Imperial's home, By The Name! There was no place for malefactors here.

"Come," the Ja'pah finally said, springing up from his chair. Perhaps he had also become impatient. Did they not want to acknowledge us? That would be typical of high-caste. They probably wanted to award us, but not in front of the holoscreen. Who would want to recognize a master criminal? And besides, the Ja'pah didn't participate in publicity.

As soon as we stepped from the ship, guards surrounded us. I saw guards by two other ships as well and recognized the Blue, Red and Green cloaks of the Minions near them. The Ja'pah waved his hand, and all the guards stood still and quiet, like I had frozen the guard during the Isdol cate. We walked past them with ease.

Maheir Ja'pah, Reso mentally projected as the three Minions joined behind us. *Was that necessary?*

Voice spoke out loud for my mate, "We've waited long enough."

More guards came to block us, but they were frozen as well as we moved down halls with ceilings meters high, sculptures jutting out from the walls, and large paintings hanging down from crystal poles. Again, just like at The Lady's home, I barely had time to take in the magnificence of the place.

I walked in the same row with the Minions, just a few steps behind the Ja'pah, when we approached the grand doors of the ballroom. The doors were open, held by two large statues representing Imperial TeNeil and his mate, Rasendei. Thousands of voices floated through the doorway, and we walked straight toward them. There were side staircases leading to the balconies, but we passed these and headed straight to the grand floor.

The buzzing voices and lulling music increased as we walked on the marble floor. Then, the music suddenly stopped and the voices turned to exclamations and whispers as soon as we became visible to everyone in the ballroom--all the high-castes of the Four Quadrants.

The Imperial and his family snugly sat on the large platform opposite from us, but their eating table was not in front of them. They must have all just finished their feast, a feast to which we were not invited. The Grand Queen Holen floated above in her usual quiet place. Even reserved, she looked full of might.

Guards flooded the room and stood in front of the royal family, lining all the sides of the grand floor. My heart pounded relentlessly as we stopped our march. Hushes fell like waves over the room as everyone become silent in anticipation of what would be said.

Voice came from behind the Ja'pah and stood slightly ahead of him. "Greetings, Imperial TeNeil," he bowed and then to the Imperial's mate. "Imperialness. Please forgive our brusque entrance."

Someone moved on the platform, and I immediately noticed Vortsi and The Lady herself, right next to him. I was right. The announcement had already been made. They had probably stated that Vortsi's rescuers wanted to remain anonymous.

The Imperial's Voice took several steps forward, his long golden gown sweeping the floor, highlighting his many wrinkles enfolded in his paper-soft skin. In an awe-inspiring voice, the short being said, "Your reputation precedes you, Ja'pah. But you will not be honored highly here."

I stared at Vortsi, who stood and said nothing.

Voice looked around and moved his hooded head back in the Imperial's speaker's direction. "It is not honor that we seek, Imperial. It is union. Your domain and mine."

The Imperial's guests guffawed at this requests, dismissing him like a lowly worm. When they settled down, The Imperial's Voice announced, its short arms spread out towards the guests in the ballroom, "You have your answer. Such a request is preposterous. We will not have any dealings with such a Being. Your evils outweigh your goods, Ja'pah." He emphasized his last sentence, and I knew he had us cornered. The Imperial didn't have to admit that it was the Ja'pah who had aided his cousin in capturing his mate. No one needed to know, and who would believe it otherwise?

"Then you reject our request," Voice's tone was low, almost daring.

"You have our answer," the Imperial's Voice looked as if he held back a sinister grin.

"Very well, then," Voice bowed and walked back to his position, aligning himself with his brothers and myself, who stood behind the Ja'pah.

"Then perhaps," the Ja'pah spoke then, his awesome voice reverberating through the air in the room, "you would accept," he took several steps forward and simply stated, "the request from your own son."

Questions ran through the audience like rolling clouds, and then accusations of blasphemy. The Ja'pah, unaffected by the thousands of voices, took off his hood and dropped his cloak to the ground.

The shouts of curses and insults that ran through the air struck me so hard that I stumbled back. Reso was at my side immediately, as I felt a large weight being lifted from my body, and electrifying energy shoot through me. I had never felt so much power, so much force in my entire life. It blinded me from the figure that stood in front of me for several moments before I could recover. So much power. So much force!

The large Wendh who was positioned where the Ja'pah once stood was completely unclothed. The presence that I had seen when Vortsi stepped out of the black capsule exploded from this Being tenfold. Thick cords of cartilage ran in parallel alignment from his forehead to the back of his neck and dangled down his back. His black skin glistened from oil and was taut around his muscles. Suddenly, his tentacles sprang out, all six of them, and several members of the crowd stood up as if to run in panic before silence swept over the room. The Wendh's extra arms began to move, swinging high in the air. They flew about so fast that they emitted a high-pitched tone. As I watched, the arms' movement seemed to blur together in a black mass, flying about so fast that it looked like . . . it formed what seemed like . . . .

"Wings!" someone shouted, and screams sputtered the air. Some guests pointed, their voices filled with violent threats and accusations, while others fell to their knees, filling the ballroom with praises and exultations.

Chaos ran through the house of Imperial TeNeil.

"Silence!" a thundering voice sliced through the fold, and the Imperial stood up, his eyes glossy with threats and fury.

The crowd gradually calmed down, though mutterings still persisted.

Imperial TeNeil came down from the platform, pushing guards out of his path as he made his way to the Wendh, who looked like the image on the talisman that millions of Beings displayed on their chests. He stopped and stared into the face of this Wendh who stood naked on his grand floor, and I thought for a moment that he wanted to slash the Being's throat.

"How dare you," the Imperial's voice whispered, though all could hear clearly in this acoustically perfect room. "How dare you patronize my son's--"

"TeNeil." Rasendei stood up, glistening from the light reflecting from the crystal-flesh that toppled her head.

TeNeil turned around as all watched the Imperialness gracefully descend the platform's steps and walk up to the Wendh whose appearance caused discord in her home. She circled the male, who lowered his flying tentacles and stopped their mass whirling, and her eyes gleamed. When she had reached the front of him again, she put her hand to his face and cupped his cheek. The emotion that filled her face was clear to all--a mother's grief released.

"My son." Her voice choked on the words as her body trembled with saddened joy.

TeNeil could not relinquish his anger as he stared questionably at his mate. She turned to look at him. "Open your mind, my husband, this male is your son."

He wouldn't hear of it. "If he is our son, why did he not return home after the war? Why become this," he waved his hand at the cloak bundled on the floor, "this *thing*?"

I saw his heart breaking, and I knew he knew that the Ja'pah was his son. But how could an Imperial accept such a creature as his own blood?

"Because he had to!" A crackling voice said from above. All eyes turned in stunned awe at the Grand Queen Holen. Never before had she uttered a word in the lifespan of everyone in this room. She floated her great chair down to the floor and lifted herself up, using her staff for support. Even at her age, she did not look much older than the two royal bloods who stood in front of the Ja'pah.

"Do you think he would have been able to complete his task living in this place?" she crackled, hobbling only slightly as she approached. "You can't get anything accomplished here! Too rosy; too cozy." Scooting the Imperialness away from her son, she clapped the naked Wendh on his shoulder. "I know it was hard to keep away from your family, especially with those idiotic Seven Day Fests they put on every cycle." She clapped him again on his shoulder. "Well done, fledgling, well done." Turning to the Imperial, she said, "Those disgusting Xarthrens would be showing up at our doorstep, inviting themselves in, if it were not for your son, TeNeil. Taking over the Underworld was a good tactic. It's the first step in combining our forces; the only way to defeat those Xarthren things. Despite what you all may think, what you wish were true, what you foolishly make yourselves believe, they will return!"

The soft voices of the crowd gradually rose again, and I was beginning to think that the Queen was enjoying all of these shocking revelations. Her last statement was a bit too much for the crowd, and panic began to move through them.

"People!" The Lady of Isdol called to the guests as well as her own people of Isdol. "This is surely a sign." She stepped forward, he green hair swaying behind her. "My union with Vortsi is not a time for tears and rejection, as I have said before, and this new revelation of the Xarthrens has just proven what we must do." Turning towards the cameras, The Lady made a final plea to her people. "Take out the suicide chips and join the Wendhs and these people, and even the Jancso. We must reunite against a common foe or we will all perish."

The Grand Queen Holen, seeming to be in her own world, walked past the Ja'pah and Imperial and headed to me! I glanced at Reso, who gave a slight gesture with his hand to be calm. I didn't know what to do as she began yanking at my hood. She was trying to take it off, and I shyly lowered it for her.

Gasps filled the room as my cloak dropped to the floor and thousands of eyes lay on me. It was uncomfortably dignifying. All of the eyes, eyes that had once looked at me with disgust, hatred and accusations of "abomination", were now eyes of awe and bewilderment.

"Beautiful," Queen Holen complimented, as she studied my face and openly appraised my curves. "Very nice, indeed." Looking at my tiara, she tilted her head a little. "Hmph," she said, and I couldn't quite make out what she meant by that. Did she recognize Tokie?

The Queen grabbed my hand suddenly with a grasp that made me wince. "Come on, child. Let your mate's parents get a good look at you."

I tried not to stumble as she presented me to the Imperial and his mate, and Rasendei actually bowed to me. To me! I didn't know what to say or do. This was all happening so fast.

I was finally relieved from all the enthralled eyes as the Imperial announced, "So it appears that you are indeed my son." His voice was still filled with some disbelief. He then added, a little disquieted, "I can feel the power in you and your mate, a power that seems to exceed my own."

The crowd reacted again to that disclosure, and the Imperial, filled with agitation, suddenly commanded, "Silence!" shocking the anxieties out of the high-caste guests. Looking around before resting his eyes back on the Ja'pah, he quietly acknowledged him. "LaSar, my son, we have some quiet discussions to attend to." With that, he waved his hand to the side, beckoning the Wendh with Wings to pass ahead of him, which was a spectacular honor.

My mate, LaSar, the youngest child of Imperial TeNeil and Imperialness Rasendei, mentally clothed himself with his cowl, allowing his head to remain uncovered, and stepped forward towards the royal platform to the door behind the throne, his parents behind him.

"Introductions are over," Queen Holen said, releasing her hard grip around my hand. She then floated back up in her chair and exited from a window high above, her usual grand exit from the ballroom. The rest of the Imperial's family headed out the door where the Imperial had exited.

The orchestra began playing again and the crowd, as well as I and the Minions, stood around, trying to figure out what to do next.

"Please continue your merriment," the Imperial's speaker announced, as if nothing amazing had just taken place, and took his seat back on the platform.

I turned to look at Voice for directions, and Reso bent down and took my cloak, draping it around his arm.

Back to the ship? Voice projected to his brothers and me. *Jetticia, please lead the way.*

We made our exit with the Minions following me as if I were of Imperial royal blood; but as soon as we past the grand ballroom doors, we were stopped by a female Joya with a brown-and-black feathered head and surrounding guards.

"I will show you to your quarters," she bowed with earnest humbleness.

I didn't know what to do next, and the Minions seemed to be following my lead. I decided to accept her offer, considering that going to the ship was not an option anyway. We followed her through large hallways, and this time I was able to see the richness of the palace. I was sure that one hallway of items alone could make me live comfortably for the rest of my lifetime.

We were taken to small hover cars to cover the great expanse of the palace and stopped inside a parlor. Here, we were separated, and I felt vulnerable.

"Their rooms are connected to yours through the parlor," the Joya explained, which put me at ease. I could call to them at any moment and they would be there.

Four Xen servants came to undress and bathe me, which was quite an unexpected, pleasing gesture. I quickly became accustomed to the aid and the feel of the soft fur of the Xen as I reverted back to the ways of my home world. Most buildings, even the elaborate ones, were the do-it-yourself kind and used an electronic host; I would use Bymé to connect with the appliances of the rooms.

One of the servants took off my tiara while I bathed, and I cautiously watched her place it on a nearby table. I was sure Tokie was anxious to transform and talk about the events that had just transpired, but for now, she had to play her part and wait until the servants left.

Food was brought in after the washing, and it was all that I imagined royal and high-caste Beings of the Four Quadrants would eat. It was also adjusted to my particular tastes. I ate slowly, with my eyes closed.

I think I could get use to this, I mentally projected to Voice, making sure I could still speak to him.

You should, he answered. *For your protection, as well as the Ja'pah, this is going to be your new home from now on.*

I gave him a mental smile.

This was all going right, but my smile faded as I glanced back at the table where the tiara had been placed and saw that it was gone.

Tokie!

What is it? Voice questioned.

Tokie's gone! I glanced accusingly at the maids, who stood by in case I needed something.

It wasn't them, Voice picked up my projections of blame. *It would mean their deaths if they were thieves like you.* He sent a calming smile along with his joke. *She's probably out exploring.*

I knew she shouldn't have come, I grimaced.

She's very useful.

I frowned. *Useful for getting into trouble.*

# # #

Tokie returned when I was half asleep. I swear she was born to irritate the world.

"Politics," she jumped on the bed, jerking me into wakefulness. "Just boring, political politics."

"Where have been? And don't ever do that again," I reprimanded her. "You could jeopardize us."

"Too late." She popped something in her mouth that I couldn't see. "LaSar told them everything, and that's when I made my appearance, but I appeared only after I watched the arguments of 'if the Xarthrens were actually returning or not.'

They finally decided to begin preparing for vengeful insects just in case." She giggled. "Nonetheless, the royal family is back on the correct path, and I am satisfied. But then they started into politics again, and discussions of apprehending The Lady's cousin Yolikeg, and other stuff which was utterly boring, so I left."

I rubbed my still-sleepy eyes. "So, they know what you are?" I was sure she had to explain herself.

"Of course not!" She popped something else in her mouth, which I saw was candy. "Don't be ridiculous, Jetticia, that story isn't ready to be told yet. And," she jumped off the bed, "this story has just finished. Not as exciting as your mother's, mind you, but it will do." I bit my tongue at the insult and rolled my eyes as she laughed.

In the middle of her laughter she said, "So, Sage Yamar, what do you think of him?"

I blinked. That was an odd question. Why was she asking about the mysterious silver-headed Wendh back on Ytieria? "He's almost like a second father to me, why? Are you planning on returning home and annoying him?"

Her merriment snapped to a pouting seriousness. "Of course not. I've never bothered the old Wendh. Never had to before."

I raised my eyes, "Before? Why do you have to now?" Something was amiss.

Tokie shrugged. "Oh, I'm not going to right now. Maybe later." She began making her way to the door, and I knew whatever she was up to, I wasn't going to get an answer . . . as always.

I sat up. "Where are you going?"

"Trang, remember?" she said, shimmering as she walked. "I have a wedding to go to. And don't worry, I'll see you again." As her light brightened, she quickly added, "You do have to admit, you enjoyed my company, even if it was . . . somewhat. .

.." She didn't finish her statement, but it could be follow by any number of words.

I didn't answer. I couldn't, anyway. She had already disappeared.

Chapter 17   The Beginning

A young, half-breed Joya sat in an abandoned building, his hands extended towards the warmth of the small fire in front of him. Next to him was an adolescent Wendh of fifteen cycles, looking over weaponry that he took out of a crate. Another youth slept, his long ears wrapped around him for comfort.

"It's over!" A voice shouted, and the sounds of scuffling feet came down the tunnel. An alluring young male with bright red hair slid into view and shouted at the two mellow youngsters. "Did you hear me? The war! It's over! We've beaten the Xarthrens!"

"Stop playing around, Vinece, we have work to do." The Wendh stood up, laying his weapon back into the crate. "Espy saw through a ship that just landed. It has a lot of cargo. It should be an easy enough job."

"But it's true! I just heard it! The word is spreading like a swarm of flying genets. It's over!"

The sleeping youth stirred awake. "Quiet, my ears." His small voice was hardly heard.

"Who else has spoken this?" Espy asked, standing up next to the fire.

Vinece went to another crate and took out some meat stuck on an iron rod. "The entire street is talking about it. All of Quuto."

"He's telling the truth," the large-eared one announced, rolling over to face them. "I can hear them."

The Wendh walked over to the sleepy youth and crouched down, whispering, "Reso, what are they saying?"

"The same thing 'The Loud One' is saying," Reso rolled back over. "The Xarthrens have been defeated and the war is over."

"See?" Vinece stuck his impaled meat into the fire. "They won't be coming here and bothering us anymore. And you, prince, can go home. It's safe now."

Reso sat up then and blinked his beady eyes in the Wendh's direction. "Leaving?"

Vinece didn't fully comprehend the words he had just said, until he recognized that statement's true meaning. His mood changed with Reso's question. For the first time, he was speechless.

The royal prince stared at his three friends, knowing what Vinece said was true--he could go home. It had been five cycles since the Xarthrens and their ship had kidnapped him and crash-landed on Quuto. Five cycles since he had seen his mother's face. Yet the idea of going home did not appeal to him. There was something he had to do, something that had been bothering him ever since he laid his eyes upon the Ja'pah two cycles ago.

The Ja'pah was full of power, power from the Underworld; it radiated with every stride he took when he disembarked from his ship. Everyone cowered in his presence and gave him respect. It was different from what he had seen around his father; it was stronger. The Ja'pah's world was strong, and the Imperial of the Underworld controlled it all with perfect orderliness. And the Ja'pah owned Quuto, a world that had now become his home, which had made him do things that would make his mother shudder just to think about it.

This life was the pattern of survival, and it seemed right.

It was then that he decided not to return home.

It was the promotion of his death that had caused the Four Quadrants to join and defeat the Xarthrens anyway. Without that symbol, the eight galaxies would be easy targets for the Xarthren when they returned. And they would return. He knew it. The Four Quadrants must be prepared, and he must be there to prepare them.

Staring again at his friends, he announced. "I'm staying."

Vinece spoke after a pause. "Staying? LaSar, are you insane? I was looking forward to the luxuries of a palace. We discussed this! Reso,

Espy and I will be a part of your house. We will gain respect and fame, and no one will look at our impureness."

Reso interjected. "Being half-breeds is not a curse by Suphyz."

Vinece turned on Reso, enraged. "It is for me! I have no place to live, no place to go. Quuto, home of half-breeds. This place is not where I am meant to be!"

The prince agreed, shocking the three in front of him. "No, you're right. This is not where you should be."

As the three youths stared at him as LaSar bent back down toward the crate and took out a weapon with a sharp edge, and then went to another crate and took out a bowl and a bottle of water. Cutting himself, he allowed his blood to trickle into the metal bowl and then poured water into it.

Extending the bowl to his friends, he intoned, "I make you all a part of me," and then, pointing the bowl, to The Loud One, he announced, "Vinece, be my Voice." "Espy," he continued, extending the bowl to the half-Joya, "You be my Eyes," and finally, pointing to the long-eared youth, he softly said, "Reso, you be my Ears."

The three stared, too stunned to make a sound until Reso broke the silence. "Your blood, LaSar, is not to be taken lightly. Do you know what power you will be giving us? We are not worthy."

The Prince continued to hold out the bowl to them. "If I am to become the Ja'pah and save the Four Quadrants from the Xarthrens' return, I will need your help."

Vinece snickered. "The Ja'pah? I knew you were a little strange, prince, with the six tentacles and all, but Ja'pah? Ti'senot, LaSar, the Xarthrens have been beaten. Did you not hear me, or should Reso repeat it for you?"

LaSar persisted. "I've seen them. They have never lost. I have been aboard their ship, and I have seen their ways. They will return, no matter how long it takes, and defeat their enemy. And when they do return, I must be in control of the Underworld in order to defeat them. My father's world was not prepared for the Xarthrens, and only my *death and propaganda prevented them from losing this war. But this world, the Underworld, was prepared. I know my father's world; they will become too confident and arrogant now and will not be prepared for another invasion. I must control this world, this Underworld, in order to help the other. So, I ask you, will you help me become Ja'pah?"*

Vinece began to laugh again. The entire concept of a royal becoming the Ja'pah was much too weird, but Espy stepped forward and took the bowl from the prince's hands. "I'll be honored to be your Eyes," he said, and sipped the watered blood, which made Vinece stop laughing.

LaSar took the bowl back and extended it to Vinece. "I can't do this without you."

Vinece hesitantly looked at Reso and Espy. "But, Ja'pah? Do you know how long that would take? Do you know what you will have to do? If you're considered one of Suphyz's favorite, an oracle or whatever, She would not ever lay Her eyes upon you again once you take this path."

LaSar answered simply. "This is my path."

Vinece seemed unconvinced, but soon shrugged. "We've been through a lot together, these five cycles. We've saved each other's lives countless times. We work pretty well for a team of thieves, and you being royal . . ." He shrugged again. They all stared at Vinece, and he looked again at the bowl. "Well, if you promise me fame and wealth, I'm yours." He walked up to the prince and took the bowl from his hands. "I will be your Voice. It's something I was half-born to do anyway." With that, he took his share of the blood.

They all turned to Reso then, who stood quietly in the flickering shadows. For a time it seemed he would object; he seemed to object to everything anyway, but then he stepped forward and took the bowl into his hands. "Someone needs to keep the sanity and wisdom in the group. I would be honored to by your Ears." Drinking down the rest of what was left in the bowl, he smiled. "So . . . let the journey begin."

# # #

Someone shook my bed in the middle of the night, waking me from the dream.

"Tokie? Back so soon?" I knew the little pest couldn't resist annoying me just one more time--

"Sorry to disappoint you," the deep voice resonated. The Ja'pah, no, LaSar, crouched over me, his face clearly visible. Large, thick cheekbones rose high and strong. His lips, thick and luscious, were slightly parted, displaying sharp, white teeth, and his large nose flared with every breath. His ears rose and pointed to the concave ceiling, while his cartilages swayed over his shoulders as he came near my face.

I had thought he would kiss my lips, a gesture only True Mates could do, else die from the toxic mix that was contained in the saliva. My father kissed my mother once, and she claimed that she saw Suphyz Herself smile down at her. Other Wendhs had expressed similar experiences with their True Mates, but I was not to have that adventure, at least not tonight.

LaSar, instead, lingered above me, taking in my face and my slowly increasing hunger. With a tip of his finger, he traced my lips and then backed away so that I could see him in full.

"I must apologize for what I have put you through," he softly said, and even more softly, his voice vibrated through the room. "There was, and is still so much to do. Your arrival was . . . unexpected." He paused to watch how I took this and slowly added, "I have become something not suitable for joining, Jetticia."

I suppressed a shiver. It was the first time he had ever said my name, and the first time I began to fear that he might reject me. That has been the case in some joinings, though very rare. After the joining was complete, the partners went their separate ways, only to reunite when the hunger became too much; but with time, the duration between such joining increased, extending to cycles. Is that what he wanted to do? Did he want to separate?

"However," that one word gave me hope, "your presence has reminded me of the Light and the comfort of Suphyz's path, a path I would very much like to return to. And this is a benefit to blessings."

I silently sighed as my tension abated, and inwardly heralded Suphyz. I guess She was right after all.

I waited for him to speak again, but when he didn't, I tried to think of something to say, yet what could you say to a statement like that? He said I was a blessing to the Ja'pah, the royal prince. It was uncomfortable to hear the Ja'pah speak that way, but it was also a comfort to know that he acknowledged me and . . . he cared.

He stopped, waiting for answer. "We are still strangers to each other, yet we have both grown from each other's presence: in strength, in wisdom, in power," he leaned forward again, pulling my blankets away. "With you by my side, the Xarthrens would be fools to return here." His breath was hot against my face when he questioned, "Do you accept this?"

Did I accept this? Where else would I rather be?

For so long I had thought Suphyz had disregarded me, but She had given me the most precious gifts that all Beings would send praises for: this place, this journey, this cate, this joining, this mate.

Reso's word echoed in my mind, You're the only kind of mixture that could mate with the Ja'pah.

A half-breed Wendh. An abomination. A mistake. Suphyz? Was this your plan for me this entire time? Was I the only Being who could mate with such a powerful Wendh? One of royalty, but a child of the Underworld. A perfect fit for an Imperial of the darknesses that resided on all worlds. I was Wendh, but half-Wendh, the only kind of Being that could accept so much of his powerful blood and live. I was his equal, but not.

I stared into the preeminent eyes of the royal prince.

Did I accept this . . .?

I breathed in deeply when he entered me, arching my back with clinched fists. Circling my arms around him, for the first time, I voluntarily touched and stroked his dark skin. It made our joining that much more, and I believed . . . that one gesture . . . was an enough of an answer for him.

The End

About the Author

Fairy Tales have always been a favorite of Deana Zhollis, along with folktales. Yet when she set her eyes on the movie Gargoyles, made in 1972 (the year of her birth), her mind's been drifting with romance, power, love and/with unearthly Beings. Mixing up her favorite things: Magic, Spirituality, the future mind, Aliens, Technology, Fairy Tales, Kisses and Fangs, the storytelling began, first with dolls and paper dolls, and on to writing Science Fiction--even before she knew what it stood for! Engulfed in the genre, she dreamed over and over of that Happily Ever After in the "adult" fashion with a twist. It's just much more fun to read for her. Living in Houston, Texas, with her dream husband, and cat Garfield, she continues her journey to imagine and write her fanciful tales.

Other Books
Ruby, Flesh and Heart

(Coming Soon...)
Feral
Elements

The Calling Series
The Made
Jetta
Creations

(Coming Soon...)
Nostrum

www.ingramcontent.com/pod-product-compliance
Lightning Source LLC
Chambersburg PA
CBHW070109260626
47160CB00004B/1384